Garden

Clubbed!

JOSH LANGSTON

*"**Garden Clubbed** is a cheeky romp through the flower beds that may crush a few of your illusions along with the petunias. Josh Langston invites you to join the ladies who take tea and talk tuberoses, but be warned: you'll never see them in quite the same way again."*

–Doris Reidy, author of the wildly popular series starring **Mrs. Entwhistle**.

This is a work of fiction. Names, characters, places, and incidents either are the product of the author's imagination or are used fictitiously, and any resemblance to any actual persons, living or dead, is purely coincidental.

ISBN 13: 978-1-732996489

More books by Josh Langston

Novels:
Resurrection Blues
A Little Primitive
A Little More Primitive
A Primitive In Paradise
Treason, Treason!
The 12,000-year-old Whisper
Oh, Bits!
Greeley
Zeus's Cookbook

Novels with Barbara Galler-Smith:
Under St. Owain's Rock
Druids
Captives
Warriors

Short Fiction:
Mysfits
Christmas Beyond the Box
Dancing Among the Stars
Who Put Scoundrels in Charge?

Textbooks on the Craft of Writing:
Write Naked!
The Naked Truth!
The Naked Novelist!
Naked Notes!

Dedication

For my wonderful sister, Karen Boyce, and not just because she's been a vocal supporter since my earliest attempts at becoming an author. She is also an amazing gardener, a loving wife, a wonderful parent, a dedicated leader, and the most genuinely nice person it has ever been my great honor to know. And if that weren't enough, she was the one who gave me the idea that sparked this book.

Thank you, KJ. This one's for you.

Contents

Acknowledgments

First Readers are a godsend. They're willing to labor through first manuscripts and root out the inevitable errors that creep into every story. Some are, by nature, capable of the finest editing skills, others simply use an abundance of God-given common sense.

Among those who helped to bring this tale to life are, in no particular order, Karen Langston Boyce, Ann Langston, John and Dee Langston, Doris Reidy, Pam Olinto, Gale McKoy, Don and Jan Wolf, and the members of my writer's groups: The Verb Mongers and the Soleil Critters.

I'm indebted to all of you for your invaluable assistance.

Chapter One

"Whatever women do they must do twice as well as men to be thought half as good. Luckily this is not difficult."
– Charlotte Whitton

Everyone agreed, the Hildegard Henderson Horticultural Award had to be the most bizarre, garish, and wholly undesirable trophy ever conceived. Standing just over four feet tall, it was unrivaled for its tasteless use of semi-precious gems, jewelry grade metals, and hand-blown glass from the famed island of Murano in Venice, Italy. How someone had managed to assemble so many lovely things into something so incontestably hideous was a question only the late founder of the St. Charlotte Garden Club could answer.

Sadly, the trophy's namesake had gone on to that horticultural haven in the hereafter before she'd taken the time to explain what her second-in-command daintily referred to as "diddly squat."

Ramona Dorn, newly elevated leader of the middle Georgia club, paced slowly around the alleged prize making little clicking noises with her tongue, just as most of the other club members had. The object of their concern sat on a velvet-clad pedestal near the front of the club's meeting space, the so-called "grand ballroom" of the Charles County Convention Center. The Center, also home to the Kiwanis, the Junior League, and every other social and/or civic club in the county, occupied the remains of the former Dew Come Inn near the edge of town where a fire had conveniently eliminated the motel's rooms. The only structure still standing had been unattached to the main building and thus escaped the conflagration unscathed.

Ramona closed her eyes and uttered a silent prayer, asking the Almighty for enough strength to see her through the rest of her term as Acting President of the club, a job she had never sought and one which could not end soon enough.

"Ramona, dear," breathed Constance DuBois, the club's resident expert on all things gossip worthy, "have all the terms of the contest been finalized? There's a nasty little rumor going 'round about—"

"Please, Connie. Stop. I'm doing the best I can to pull this thing together. I don't need anyone spreading tales about anything right now."

"Well," coughed the matronly club member. "I certainly hope you're not referring to me!"

"I'm speaking in generalities," Ramona said, not wanting to become a target for one of the club's worst verbal manure spreaders. "As far as I can tell, the rules are set in stone."

"But—"

"Make that granite. Titanium, maybe."

Constance bristled. "That's not a stone."

"Right. But you get the idea."

"I s'pose," she said, breathing out in a prolonged hiss. "And once again, Hildegard Henderson gets her way."

Ramona shrugged. "That's one way to look at it. She could have left her money to—"

"The membership?"

"I was going to say 'charity.' An orphanage or something." With her eye on the overly made-up rumor monger at her side, Ramona thought perhaps a clown college would have been a more worthy recipient.

Constance continued, "It just seems like our dear departed leader might have found a better use for her wealth than this ridiculous contest and..." She paused for breath, as if the room's air had been tainted by the presence of the trophy. "That... thing."

"And yet," Ramona said, "a lot of our members intend to compete for it. Especially the younger ones."

Constance limited herself to a soft grunt. What remained unspoken, by them and most of the other garden clubbers, was the other half of the award, the real reason so many wanted the prize.

~*~

Sheila Moran tried not to look too obvious as she stared at the garden club trophy in front of her. All but dripping with jewels, the prize which had drawn so much disdain from the other club members looked like a gift from God to her. She had to have it. Hoping to remain somewhat discreet when taking cellphone snapshots of the prize, she kept her mobile device at hip level throughout the process. With any luck, one or more of the photos would capture the trophy in depth and give her the opportunity to examine it at her leisure.

3

As one of the newest club members, Sheila had yet to meet many of the others. She'd grown up in a suburb of Atlanta, but most of the club members seemed to be locally grown. Profound Southern accents were the rule rather than the exception. While Atlanta had become more and more cosmopolitan, St. Charlotte retained—and prided itself—on its rural roots.

Though the club considered its primary goals to be garden-oriented, in reality it served a very different function—to provide a social outlet for its many participants. One simply had to join the clique or face the prospect of being a social outcast. Sheila's interests, however, were more fiduciary than floral. Having influential friends, especially those with conspicuous wealth, could provide a multitude of options for someone like her. She had learned early in life that ethics were fine, provided they didn't get in one's way.

Sheila loved the sparkle of all the little gems on the trophy. Though not classically trained, she could spot a valuable stone as well as any jeweler, and this monstrous compilation of Tiffany flotsam offered more than its share. Best of all, if she won it, nobody would expect to see it again before the following year's competition for it began. Her devious little mind whirled with possibilities.

More pragmatist than optimist, Sheila also realized she'd need nothing less than a Herculean effort to create a competitive garden, a task made even more daunting by the fact she knew nothing about plants. Her horticultural knowledge was limited to a corsage from a high school suitor and a few bouquets gleaned from various romantic adventures.

She refused, however, to let that little detail stand in her way. In fact, she had already begun to form a plan.

4

~*~

William Broome, known as "Bubba" to most townsfolk, held the title of Site Manager for the Charles County Convention Center. The CCCC, while not a huge building, did provide a non-denominational setting for just about anything and anyone other than the annual 4H Club's Livestock Show. Bubba's current job entailed many of the same duties he'd had as the former manager of the Dew Come Inn, plus any required maintenance. No one could prove he had anything to do with the fire, although his uncle, Odell Odum, the town Sheriff, had questioned him soundly, a process which took nearly a half hour, after which the two went out for lunch.

Bubba watched with more than a casual eye as the garden club ladies ambled slowly around the grand prize as if viewing the guest of honor at a circus funeral. Though their expressions appeared suitably dour, many engaged in animated discussions once they ventured near the back of the room. Most of those chats seemed focused on the mental stability of the trophy's creator and/or the woman who had funded it. The chats which garnered most of his attention were those that touched on the materials that went into the award's construction. This included silver and more than a few bits of gold, to say nothing of gemstones. All of which coalesced in his mind as one thing: unburied treasure.

"Just getting by," at the ripe old age of twenty-five, was a lifestyle Bubba struggled to accept. A little treasure could go a long way toward changing that lifestyle into something far more desirable. But dreams of unbridled wealth weren't the only things to occupy his mind as he eyed the procession of females giving the grand prize their critical review. He'd always thought garden clubs were the exclusive province of old ladies, and yet if the parade in the ballroom was any indication, this club had plenty of younger members. Some, no more than a few years his senior, could have held their own in any number of beauty contests. A lifelong fan of bathing suit competitions, he'd never missed one available on his TV screen. More than once he'd thanked God for cable.

Bubba wiped his forehead with a sleeve. He wasn't used to having his imagination fired so acutely.

~*~

Once Ramona ended the meeting and disengaged from a gaggle of garden clubbers asking questions she'd already answered a half dozen times, she made her way home and poured herself a queen-sized glass of much-needed wine. It wasn't a great vintage, not that she cared. The selection at the local Piggly Wiggly left something to be desired, but it met her needs. Feet up and glass in hand, she closed her eyes and relaxed for what seemed like the first time since hearing of Hildegard Henderson's passing. Hildie had been in excellent health, but Ramona never asked her about her desire to visit potentially dangerous places. Clearly, that had been a strategic blunder. She now felt she had little choice but to honor her reluctant pledge to serve as the club's primary officer.

"We've needed someone younger for quite a while," Hildie had said. "We need someone with new ideas, new ways of thinking, and new ways of getting things done."

Ramona had serious doubts about the club's willingness to do *anything* differently, much less new. That included any thinking process which hadn't evolved during the club's century-plus existence. With that in mind, she'd agreed to serve as the organization's Vice President, a position she hoped would carry few, if any, responsibilities.

Ramona didn't regret joining the organization, though

her original intent had nothing to do with socializing, much less learning about shrubs and flowers, or—God forbid—vegetables. She simply wanted to help secure new clients for her son's burgeoning landscape business. Young Donny was earnest and kindhearted but lacked the killer instinct Ramona assumed lay at the heart of any commercial venture.

Donny faced stiff competition. St. Charlotte had more landscapers than one might reasonably expect to find in a Southern country town of middling size. Much to her surprise, however, Donny did reasonably well, especially after he brought some of his college pals on board. Muscular and athletic, Donny's crews usually worked bare-chested during the warmer months, and while many of the garden club ladies commented on it, few ever complained.

Ramona had no idea Hildie even knew who Donny was, so it came as a distinct shock when she discovered Hildie had included a paid-up subscription for Donny's services as the other half of the annual award for her namesake competition. In addition to "ownership" of the garish trophy, this amounted to ten hours of landscape-related labor, per week, for a calendar year to be provided by Donny and/or one of his workers. Materials were not included.

The only conclusion Ramona could draw from this was that Hildie had guaranteed her award would be sought after, at least for as long as Donny hired healthy young studs to do the grunt work.

Grunt work. The irony made her laugh. She had to admit, though sneaky, old Hildie was successful, and Ramona admired that. Some of the younger members would be all in for the laborers, and maybe even some of the labor, while the older members would be assured of having plenty to talk about. A win-win if there ever was one.

~*~

Once home, Sheila had the opportunity to examine her snapshots. She took her time with the study.

The trophy, she assumed, was meant to resemble a garden trowel stuck blade-down in a pail, both of which were apparently fashioned from silver. The handle of the over-sized trowel, along with the "topsoil" in the bucket, were littered with sparkly gems. Surrounding the pail and trowel were long, slender stems of gold supporting glass blossoms in various colors. Sheila assumed there was some correlation between the glass blooms and those which occurred in nature, but she couldn't be sure. That was a gardener thing, and she was hardly a gardener.

Given enough time, she figured she could duplicate the entire thing in faux gems and silver plate. With any luck, she'd be long gone before anyone noticed the switch. She'd have the gold and silver melted down and the gemstones neatly separated by size, weight, and clarity. She doubted any were so valuable that they carried identifying marks; those were usually reserved for jewelry grade stones. That didn't mean the ones in the trophy were worthless. On the contrary, due to their volume, she anticipated raking in enough from their sale to cover the last of the cosmetic surgeries she'd endured over the years.

Then, too, there was always the possibility of connecting with a buyer who wouldn't recognize a real diamond if it cut open his heart. She'd sold distinctively cut glass to more than a few such morons who were only too happy to trust her. At least while she hung around and willingly sat in their laps, a situation which wouldn't last too long if she could just win the stupid gardening contest.

At first, she decided she didn't need a crooked jeweler

as much as she needed a crooked gardener, preferably a male with deep pockets. Sadly, they didn't tend to advertise. Then she realized her best bet would be to find someone single who already had a spiffy garden. Love, or the semblance of same, could solve a world of problems.

~*~

"There were some babes in there I tell ya. I never woulda guessed." Bubba Broome knocked the water off the coaster formerly under his beer and put it back in place. Odell Odum sat across from him in the town's most colorful if least affluent bar, the Deep Six. Owing to the usual beer-drinking clientele, most locals referred to it as the Six Pack.

"No kidding? Some of the garden club gals *aren't* on Social Security?"

"That's a fact." Bubba took a long sip of his brew. "I ain't sayin' there weren't some granny types there, 'cause there were. Lots of 'em. But there were some really fine-lookin' ladies in there, too."

"Cougars."

"Huh?"

Odell offered up a modest belch. "One of my deputies got a part-time job as a server at the garden club's annual dinner. He claims a couple of those gals hit on him."

Bubba's interest level spiked. "No kidding?"

Odell shrugged. "I've not reason to doubt him."

Bubba sat back in the wooden booth, his mind clearly wandering. "Imagine that. A room full of lonely women."

"So," continued Odell, "tell me about this trophy you called me about. What's so special about it?"

9

"It's gotta be worth a fortune!" Bubba gushed. "The thing weighs a ton, I swear. I had to lift it up and set it on some kinda pedestal. Thought I'd get a hernia or something."

"Gotta use your legs."

"I *did* use my legs!"

"Okay, so it's heavy. What else?"

Bubba bobbed his head as he talked and waved his hands as if to weave more meaning into his words. "It stands about yay high," he said, with his flattened hand at belt level, "and it looks kinda like a bucket and a shovel. A small one, y'know?"

"You mean a *trowel*? Like a gardener would use?"

"Exactly!"

"Imagine that," said Odell, trying to put a look of wonder on his face. "A gardening tool used in a gardening award. I'm astonished someone could come up with something like that."

Bubba's expression betrayed confusion. "Anyway, that part—the biggest part—looks like it's made outta silver. But it's got a whole bunch of diamonds, rubies, sapphires, and I dunno what else stuck to it. Gotta be worth... geez, I dunno how much. A lot, that's for sure."

"All that stuff might just be for show, y'know," Odell said. "Most every trophy I've ever seen was made of plastic. But you say this one's heavy?"

"Oh Lord, yes. Plus, it's got gold flower stems stickin' out of it."

"Out of the bucket?"

"Around the edges."

"How do you know they're flower stems?"

"'Cause they've all got pretty glass flowers attached to the ends."

"*Glass* flowers?"

"Yeah."

"Seems a bit much," observed Odell. He accepted the bar tab and set it beside his empty glass. "Y'know, Bubba, your Momma and I were pretty close. And Lord knows I miss her more than anybody, 'cept maybe you."

Bubba's head drooped slightly, but he remained silent.

"And I've prob'ly told you this a thousand times, but I promised her I'd keep an eye on you. Keep you outta trouble."

"More like a million times."

Odell squinted at him. "Don't be a jerk."

"Sorry."

"I'm your uncle, not your daddy. But he ain't around anymore either, so I reckon I'll have to do."

"Why don't you just go ahead and say what's on your mind," Bubba said. "I can't sit here all night."

Odell exhaled heavily. "Just promise me you won't do anything stupid."

"Like what?"

"Like tryin' to steal that ugly old trophy."

"Never said I would."

"You didn't have to."

"But—"

Odell left a twenty on the table and got up to leave. "I

11

may run the jail, son, but I can't keep you out of it if you're bound and determined to spend time in there."

~*~

News about the club's contest, and the visible part of the prize, had circulated for some time. The *Chatter*, St. Charlotte's local newspaper and Ramona's former employer, had carried the story accompanied by photos of the award. Unfortunately, the article hadn't mentioned her son's landscaping company, which would have been a lovely bit of free advertising.

Ramona still had to provide all the details in the club's newsletter, something she'd been editing since she joined the club two years earlier. After the divorce, she found too much free time on her hands, and when the club learned about her work with the *Chatter*, they were only too eager for her to manage their publication, *The Blossom*. Ramona hated the title, and remembered when she suggested to Hildie that it be changed. The response was laughter.

"The name of the newsletter is that big of a deal?"

"I don't care for it either," Hildie said, "but the membership would rebel if we tried to change it. My plan has always been to introduce new ideas and new things to do. If we're smart, we won't have to change any of the old things."

Ramona nodded. "And pray the old habits just die out?"

Hildie smiled. "You got it! They have a name for it in football. Leonard, my husband, is always using it." She tapped her temple lightly as she searched her memory. "Now I remember. He calls it an 'end around.' I'm not sure what that means in football, but it sure sounds like what I had in mind."

Ramona had endured too many fall weekends dominated by televised football and her ex-husband's devotion to it. His unwillingness to step away from a game on the tube for anything, including their anniversary, was but one of the reasons their marriage had fallen apart. "I hate football," she said.

"I don't!" Hildie said with a laugh. "I can get a lot more done when Leonard's glued to the TV. He must have a dozen 'favorite' teams. I don't know how he keeps 'em straight. But the main thing is, when there's a game on, he forgets I'm there."

"And that's a good thing?"

"When you've been married as long as I have," Hildie said, "that's a great thing. Besides, I know what he's really interested in."

"You do?"

"Oh, sure. It's the cheerleaders. But as long as he's drooling over them on television, I don't have to worry about him drooling over them somewhere else." She chuckled. "Not that any self-respecting cheerleader would have anything to do with the old goat."

~*~

Prior to her 55th birthday, Hildie Henderson had never considered her life or any plans for it in terms of phases. That all changed the following day, and her life veered in a completely different direction.

Phase One had largely been completed. It had taken over a year and a great deal more effort than she at first imagined, but it had been worth it. Though she had started slowly with twice weekly yoga classes, she quickly realized that wouldn't be nearly enough to reach her goals. So, she arranged to attend classes daily using three different instructors. When she advanced faster and farther than her classmates, she was forced to find new classes and new instructors.

Her fitness regimen didn't end with yoga, however. She also hired a personal trainer who oversaw her nutrition and weight training programs. And, as if all that weren't enough, she also took classes in self-defense.

The revelation that caused all this had been a long time coming. Hildie's husband, Leonard, had always been a good provider. He ran a local accounting firm, and she was content to be a homemaker. They had never been blessed with children.

Hildie had never given much thought to their financial circumstances, as Leonard took care of everything. Little changed in their first two decades together; Leonard did whatever accountants did, and Hildie gardened. And then one day, Leonard announced they were moving to a bigger house. Her input toward this decision had not been sought. The deal was done; they were moving.

Losing her beloved garden had been difficult, but Leonard agreed to foot the bill for anything she wanted to do in their new residence. Once she had an opportunity to explore the potential of their new home and expansive lot, her attitude changed. She would create a bigger and better place of beauty than she'd left behind.

Over the next few years, she concentrated not only on her garden, but the gardening needs of the club members with whom she'd become good friends. And while she was certainly aware of some extravagant changes to the lifestyle Leonard provided, she assumed he was merely reaping the rewards of his keen, mathematical mind and matchless attention to detail.

Until shortly after that 55th birthday, she had no idea he was laundering money for a drug cartel, or that he had a girlfriend about half Hildie's age.

Chapter Two

"Being a woman is a terribly difficult task since it consists principally in dealing with men." – Joseph Conrad

Willa Mae Sundee, head of the Charles County Garden Club, saved her copy of *The Chatter* in which she first learned of the city club's new contest. She had examined the article with care, hoping to find a complete set of rules, but such was not the case. Nor had she been able to determine if the rival club intended to let non-members compete.

The St. Charlotte organization, often referred to by her friends as the Saint Charlatans, or just the "townie" club, had been around nearly twice as long as Willa Mae's club. Nevertheless, she and her fellow members took great pride in their accomplishments. For the past fifty years or so, members of the much smaller rural club had claimed claim most of the blue ribbons from the floral competitions at the annual Charles County Fair. The townies fared even worse when it came to vegetables. Willa Mae secretly hoped they'd try their hands at livestock someday.

When it came to growing things, the townies, with all their money and all the paid help they could ever want, would never catch up to their country neighbors. Nothing pleased Willa Mae more, even if the stuck-ups in St. Charlotte never admitted it. So, when she realized there might be a new way to showcase her club's superiority, she couldn't wait to get the details.

When *The Chatter* failed to provide the necessary information, Willa Mae had no choice but to call her counterpart in town. Communication between the two organizations had been limited and, at best, stilted. Willa Mae worried that remarks made by some of her fellow club members after the last county fair might have damaged relations even further. Sadly, some folks just took gardening too seriously.

"This is Willa Mae Sundee," she said into her cell phone, trying to sound upbeat. "May I please speak to Mrs. Henderson?"

She heard a sigh on the other end, followed by a brief silence. "I'm afraid that's impossible," said the man who answered the phone. "Hildie, my wife... She, uh, passed away."

"Oh, dear," Willa Mae said, biting her lip. "I had no idea. I'm so sorry to hear that." *Great. Now I have to find out who's taken her place.* "I was hoping to talk to her about the gardening contest she was sponsoring. Is that still on?"

"As far as I know," said the man. "I don't get involved in that stuff."

"I see. Do you have any idea who I might call instead?"

"You might talk to Bubba over at the Dew Come Inn, or what's left of it. That's where the club met."

"Bubba *owns* the place?" She knew several males who

answered to that name, but she felt sure she didn't know this one.

"He takes care of it. Decent guy, supposedly, or so I hear. He might be able to help."

"Thanks," she said and cut the connection.

Eventually, Willa Mae got in touch with Bubba who gave her Ramona Dorn's name and number. She likened the process to a tooth extraction without a painkiller.

"Mizz Dorn? I'm Willa Mae Sundee. I'm calling on behalf of—"

"I hate to admit this," said the woman on the phone, "but I'm completely out of money for charity this year."

"—the Charles County Garden Club," said Willa Mae.

Both women remained silent for a moment and then chuckled. Willa Mae said, "May I please speak with Ramona Dorn?

"That's me," Ramona said. "I apologize. I—"

"Don't give it a thought. I'm tired of charity calls, too. Seems like they never stop."

"How can I help you?" Ramona asked.

Willa Mae plowed ahead. "I have a question or two about the new gardening contest. I read about it in the paper and tried to call Mrs. Henderson, then learned she had passed away."

"It's a tragedy," Ramona said. "Hildie was a wonderful person."

"Had she been ill?"

"Oh, gosh no. She was the picture of health. She was a good ten years older than me, but went to yoga class several times a week. I wish I had that kind of drive and stamina."

"So, what happened to her?"

"No one's quite sure," Ramona said. "She was on a cruise with friends and went missing somewhere in Israel. Or maybe it was Turkey. I don't know. Somewhere in the Middle East."

"How perfectly awful." Willa Mae tried to imagine being stranded in the Third World. "Is it possible she's still alive, but trapped somewhere?"

"It doesn't seem likely. They found her things in her cabin on the boat, but no signs of her or of foul play. She just seems to have disappeared. Her memorial service was well attended, and I'm pretty sure there was an article in the paper about it." Ramona paused. "Some folks think she may have gone overboard."

"*Seriously?* That's terrible! I guess that means you'll cancel the contest."

"Actually, no. Hildie had the whole thing set up before she went on her trip."

"Even the name?"

"Yep. After all, she donated the money for it. I'm told she even mentioned it in her will: the Hildegard Henderson Horticultural Award. She thought it had a nice ring to it."

Willa Mae squirmed. "She really named it after herself? That's kinda— I dunno—weird, isn't it?"

"That's not for me to say. But I know you didn't call to chat about that."

"Nope. I called hoping to get more information about the contest. The paper didn't say if it was open to anyone or just members of your club." Willa Mae held her breath waiting for an answer.

"I don't know if Mrs. Henderson had an opinion about that."

Oh, so it's Mrs. Henderson now. No more Hildie. "Can I get a copy of the rules?"

"I don't see any harm in that," Ramona said. "They're in the club newsletter, but they may not be complete. How 'bout I mail you a copy?"

"I'm willing to drop by and pick one up," Willa Mae said. "Several of my club members are quite interested."

"Well, if you insist. I should be home for the rest of the day." She gave Willa Mae her street address and cautioned her about some work being done on the streets in her neighborhood.

"Thank you so much," Willa Mae said. "I'll see you later today."

~*~

Bubba had just finished mowing the strip of grass between the Convention Center and County Road 11 which connected downtown St. Charlotte with the interstate highway. The strip seemed to have more litter and weeds than grass, but Bubba dutifully leveled it all with the bush hog attachment on the back of a small tractor borrowed from his uncle.

A car pulled into the parking lot as he got off the tractor and prepared to go inside for something cold to drink. He was pretty sure he'd left a beer or two in the 'fridge and frowned when he saw a matronly old lady get out of her car and march towards him.

She called to him from a few feet in front of her late model Cadillac, "Young man!"

"Yes'm?" Bubba said as he wiped his hands on his jeans.

19

"Are you in charge here?"

He nodded assent. "Watcha need?"

"I want to discuss the security arrangements here. I'm concerned about the safety of our trophy on display inside. As you know, it's extremely valuable."

"I, uh, hadn't really noticed." Bubba shuffled his feet. "But you don't have to worry. It's plenty safe."

The woman made a huffing sound. "Do you regularly check the locks on the doors and windows? How hard would it be for someone to break in? Have you noticed anyone suspicious hanging around lately?" She paused for a breath. "These are all questions that ought to be resolved before that trophy remains in there another night."

"Well, y'see—"

"Are you here, on site, all night long? Who fills in for you when you're gone?"

Bubba's patience had grown thinner with each query. "You're the only stranger who's come 'round lately. I mean, other than the Kiwanis. They were here yesterday. I kinda like the Shriners better, what with their hats and all."

"That hardly sets my mind at ease," the woman said.

"Oh, and I got a phone call today. Some woman wanted to know about the contest rules."

"Did she give you her name?"

"Prob'ly, but I didn't write it down. I was fixin' to do my chores. Anyway, she didn't say anything 'bout comin' round here. She wanted to know if the contest was open to her club or just the folks here in St. Charlotte."

The woman frowned. "What did you tell her?"

20

"That I didn't know jack about the contest, and if she wanted information, she should call the club president. So, I gave her Miz Dorn's number."

"I see. Well, you've heard my concerns. I'm going to call Mrs. Dorn myself and make sure she understands them as well." She turned like a river barge and chugged back to her car.

Bubba relaxed. He'd faced the enemy and won. It was time for a beer.

~*~

It seemed to Ramona that no time had passed between her chat with Willa Mae and a call from Constance DuBois. Though she normally wandered around in a restrained state of high dither, Constance seemed to have amped it up for her call.

"You simply can't let those country women compete for our trophy!"

"And hello to you, too, Connie. How's it going?" Ramona instinctively rubbed her temples hoping to avoid the headache otherwise sure to come. She checked her wine glass and decided it still held enough to carry her through the conversation.

Constance didn't waver. "Surely the rules cover this. What do they say?"

"As far as I recall, the rules don't mention it."

Ramona heard Connie's sharp intake of breath followed by an explosive exhalation. "You've *got* to be kidding me!"

"Uh, nope."

"My God! This is a complete disaster."

"That's a bit of an overstatement, don't you think?" *Get a grip, Connie!*

"No! It's terrible. This is *our* award. This trophy simply must not be given to an outsider. That would be absolutely intolerable. We might never see it again."

"Now, now Connie—" Ramona found herself searching for serenity while staring at her ceiling, which, she decided probably needed a fresh coat of paint.

"Don't try to soft peddle this, Ramona. You're new on the job. I understand that. And you haven't really been a member for very long, so you don't know the other ladies like I do, but—"

"Actually, I'm on pretty good terms with them. No one's thrown vegetables at me. I take that as a good sign." She took a long sip of her wine.

"Go ahead and make light of it, but just remember, I tried to warn you."

Ramona wasn't entirely sure what she meant. "Warn me about what?"

"The—pardon my French—poop storm you'll cause if you let outsiders enter the contest. Especially those..." She lowered her voice. "Rednecks."

"Come on now, let's just think this through, okay?"

"I've said all I intend to say on the matter," Constance said, her voice frosty. "You do what you want, but don't blame me when it all blows up in your face."

The click seemed amplified when Connie hung up, as if she intended it as a last word. Ramona stared at the now-dead phone in her hand and wondered if there was any way to prevent the uproar Connie promised other than by giving in to her demands. Ramona had no strong feelings one way or the other, but there was no way she'd let a pushy, gossip-spewing, old biddy dictate policy.

It was definitely time to refill her wine glass.

~*~

Sheila Moran had certain standards when it came to seeking male company. They weren't particularly high standards, but they made sense to her. The men she looked for had to be reasonably well groomed, in at least moderately good health, and have most of their teeth. Those missing in the back didn't count. Only significant wealth could outweigh these important minimums. Sheila's pragmatism provided the bedrock of her world view, which left just about everything in her life negotiable.

Despite her standards, Sheila never had trouble connecting with men. Though not a traffic-stopping beauty, she knew how to use the attributes she had. She also knew which of her attributes would benefit from enhancement and had acted accordingly. Everything that could be surgically improved, had been.

Beauty, she discovered, was as much attitudinal as physical. Men liked women who were attractive, but they *loved* women who were fun to be with. A touch, a gesture, a look, even a self-effacing giggle, was often enough to turn a man's head. Perfect hair, perfect measurements, perfect make-up, etc. only went so far. While great for gaining a man's attention, they did little when it came to keeping it.

She could laugh at any joke and stifle any response that might be construed as flighty or uptight. Guys loved that. They could talk to her without worrying about using "bad" words or venturing into politically incorrect territory. When Sheila was on the hunt, such problematic issues simply didn't exist.

This time, however, the problem wasn't what she talked about or what she heard. She needed to find a more-or-less eligible male who already had a garden. Preferably one she could help bring to a level of elegance such that the garden club judges would fall all over themselves to award her the bejeweled prize.

As she had on other occasions, she turned her attention to the self-help groups listed ever so conveniently on the Internet. It only took a moment to find just what she needed, a local group for those grieving the loss of a loved one. After jotting down the address and meeting times, she logged off and prepared herself to be both sympathetic and charming. With any luck, she'd soon have a selection of perfectly suitable males from which to choose.

~*~

Ramona held the nearly empty wine bottle in one hand and her empty glass in the other, wondering how she could have let her supply run out. The Piggly Wiggly was still open, and since she'd only had about a glass and a half, she figured it would be safe to make the short trip and restock.

As she made her way out to the carport, she saw her son Donny pulling in, his pickup truck uncharacteristically tidy.

"Whoa!" she called as he exited the vehicle. "A clean truck? What's the occasion?"

"Well," he began, "it's uh... I've sorta got a date."

Ramona relaxed. "That's great! With who?"

"I doubt you'd know her," he said. "I only met her today."

"Okay. But tell me, what does it mean when you have a 'sorta' date. Back in the stone age, when I was dating, a date was something you either had or you didn't have. So, which is it?"

"Honestly, Mom, I'm not sure."

Ramona felt her eyebrows contract as she tried to read his face. He hadn't acted this way since the night he "sorta" hung out with some high school buddies and got caught throwing eggs at someone's house. "What aren't you telling me, Donny?"

"It's complicated."

Just the words I wanted to hear. "I may be several years out of school, but I'm way smarter than I look."

"Aw, Mom," Donny said, his voice dropping into a range and timber she hadn't heard since he was in middle school.

"Spill it, mister."

He exhaled heavily. "So, I was cleaning out a little goldfish pond this morning. It was hot, and I had my shirt off. There was a bunch of algae in it. Nasty, green stuff, even though the water was pretty clear."

"Yeah. And?"

"And the lady who owns the place kept coming outside asking me if I needed anything. You know, like water and stuff."

"What kinda stuff?"

"I dunno. She said she was worried I might get overheated."

"Were you sweating?"

"Like a pig. There wasn't a lick of shade anywhere nearby."

"So?"

"So, she practically dragged me inside her house and made me sit down and cool off."

He smiled at her as if that was the end of the story. His father had used the same tactic. It never worked for him, either. "Okay, go on."

"That's pretty much it."

Ramona laughed. "Seriously? You think I'm going to let you leave it at that? I'm still waiting to find out where the 'sorta' date comes in. Did this woman try to fix you up with her daughter or something?"

Donny's color suggested he might be hemorrhaging.

"You okay, sweetie?" she asked.

"Yeah. Look, this is a little embarrassing, okay? The lady said she wanted to get to know me better and asked if I'd go out to dinner with her tonight."

"And you said yes?"

"Yeah."

Ramona fixed him with a stare. "Is she married?"

"Maybe. I dunno."

"Don't you think it would be a good idea to find out?"

He bobbed his head like a chicken at a bonus feeding. "I... uh... didn't much think about that. I mean... Uh. Forget it. N'mind."

"Never mind what?"

"Well, she just seemed really lonely, y'know? Like she hadn't had any company in forever. I felt sorry for her, that's all."

Ramona had her suspicions but didn't voice them. "Just out of curiosity, what was this lonely woman wearing?"

"C'mon, Mom. How'm I s'posed to remember something like that?"

"Dig deep," she said, curious but expectant.

"Shorts." He closed his eyes as if straining to remember. "And uh... a T-shirt."

"Baloney!"

He looked wounded.

"What was she *really* wearing?"

"A bikini, okay? But she had a tank top over it. Kinda."

"*Kinda?*"

"Well, yeah. There wasn't much to it."

Ramona shook her head. "I don't suppose you'd care to tell me her name."

"I'd rather not."

"Listen, you're old enough to do what you like. I can't tell you who to go out with or who you should avoid. But that doesn't mean I don't care."

"I'll be fine," he said. "It's just dinner."

"Okay, but do yourself a favor," Ramona said, unable to keep herself from punctuating her thoughts with a sigh. "Keep it platonic. I don't want any grandchildren just yet."

"*What?* Hey, don't—"

He stopped talking when she held up her hand. "Save it. Go have fun. Just... Be careful, for goodness sake. Okay?"

She cruised past him and climbed into her car, more

intent than ever to purchase some wine. A case or two should do, provided she paced herself.

The parking lot at the Piggly Wiggly held few cars, which she took as a good sign. She grabbed an empty cart and pushed it back into the store—her good deed for the day.

As she perused the beer and wine aisle working left to right while a man in a police uniform did the same from the opposite direction. They had a mild collision between the Chablis and the chardonnay.

"Sorry," said the man. "Didn't mean to get in your way."

Ramona smiled. "It's my bad. I wasn't paying attention." She couldn't help but notice the Sheriff's badge on his chest. "I hope this won't go on my record."

"S'cuse me?"

She chuckled. "You know, for striking an officer."

He crossed his arms and feigned a serious expression. "I'm tempted. I haven't written anyone up all week."

Ramona felt a twinge of anxiety which evaporated when the lawman gave her a grin instead of a citation.

"I think you're safe. You didn't knock anything outta my hands. Besides, no judge on Earth would let me get away with demanding your license and registration when you're not driving."

"That's a relief," Ramona said as they both turned back to the shelves. The two nearly bumped hands while reaching for the same wine.

"Are you *trying* to get in trouble?" he asked, his lopsided smile still in place.

"It's the chardonnay's fault," she said, tilting her head at the bottle in her hand. "Although, now I'm thinking I'd be better off with an after-dinner wine. Something with a little more body."

"I know just the thing." He walked a few steps away, read several wine labels, and soon found the one he sought. He grabbed two and returned to her side. "Try this." He handed her one of the bottles.

Ramona accepted it and glanced at the label, though she would have much preferred to examine the man who'd given her the bottle. Eventually, she looked up into his eyes, and they stared at each other for what seemed like a very long and very silent moment.

"Coming through," piped a shelf stocker as he pushed a wide, heavily laden cart down the center of the aisle. "Don't wanna run over any toes."

The toe owners pressed against the shelves as he passed, and Ramona conducted a hurried inventory of her appearance. *Hair? Likely a wreck. Make-up? Probably needed work. Clothes?* Thank God she hadn't changed after the club meeting. She concluded it could've been much worse.

When the cart had safely passed, the lawman eased away. "Sorry 'bout that. Didn't mean to invade your space."

"No problem. I didn't mind." She hoped she hadn't been too forward.

"I'm Odell Odum," he said, extending his hand.

"Ramona Dorn," she replied as they concluded the obligatory ritual.

He held up his wine bottle. "I don't suppose you'd like to sit down somewhere and give this stuff a try, would you?"

Ramona couldn't help recalling her earlier conversation with Donny; she had already checked Odell's hand for a wedding band and was relieved to see only bare fingers. "Well..." *Am I crazy? I don't even know this guy!* "Uh...."

"Okay," he said. "I'm sorry. It's not like I'm prowling or anything. I just—"

"I'd love to," she said. "Have you got a place in mind?" *How dangerous could it be? He's a policeman for cryin' out loud!*

His face reflected profound relief. "There's a great little park nearby." He paused, then added, "Have you eaten? Maybe we could grab a bite of something to go with the wine."

"Wait a sec," she said. "Is it okay to drink wine in a public park? I thought—"

"I suspect we'll be just fine," he said tapping the word Sherriff on his name tag. "So, what goes well with wine?"

She grinned. "Cheese and fruit? This sounds quite romantic."

He suddenly seemed shy. "Listen, if you think this is a bad idea, we can forget it."

"No, I love the idea," she said.

"It's just— I've had a long day, and I don't feel like going home to an empty house."

"And there's nothing worth watching on the tube, right?"

He grinned. "Right."

She crooked her finger at him then turned toward the deli section. "Follow me. I know just what we need."

He quickly caught up and walked beside her. "So, what goes with red wine?"

"Just about anything," she said with a wink.

Chapter Three

"Scientists now believe that the primary biological function of breasts is to make men stupid." – **Dave Barry**

Wasting no time at all, Willa Mae bustled into her Jeep Cherokee and took off for town. She followed Ramona Dorn's instructions to the letter, pleased to have avoided the road work she'd been warned about and arrived at the address which she'd carefully taken down during their phone call.

She marched briskly up to the front door and rang the bell. A male voice from inside responded, "Be out in a minute."

Though she tried to restrain herself, Willa Mae ended up pacing back and forth on the front stoop, squeezing in two whole steps each way. Her Momma had told her more times than a normal human could count that, patience was a virtue Will Mae would have to work to develop, "'Cause she sure as heck wasn't born with it."

Eventually, a muscular young man opened the door. Wearing only a bath towel wrapped around his waist, he smiled awkwardly and said, "Sorry, I was in the shower."

"So I see," she said, forcing herself to concentrate on his face. *How long had it been since Bob looked like that?* "I—uh, just came by to pick up something from Miz Dorn. Is she around?"

"She left about the time I got home," he said. "That was maybe twenty minutes ago. I'm not sure where she went, but hang on a sec. Lemme check something."

He ducked back inside for a moment then returned. "I'm pretty sure she ran up to the grocery store. She left her glass and an empty wine bottle on the kitchen table."

"Then she should be back soon?"

"That'd be my guess," he said. "Wanna come inside?"

Though tempted, she turned away. "Thanks, but I'll wait in the car."

Willa Mae tried listening to the radio, but couldn't find a station that interested her. The news bored her; the sports stations only covered football, and her favorite music station had recently switched its format from country-western to "All talk, all the time." *What kind of idiot listens to that all day?* She concluded it had to be the townies. Most everyone she knew had more important things on their minds. Like the new gardening contest.

"That woman knew I was comin'," she told herself out loud. "I can't believe she didn't have the decency to wait 'til I showed up."

The time passed slowly, broken up only by the departure of the good-looking young man, now fully clothed, with whom she'd spoken when she arrived. He backed his sporty pickup out of the drive and waved to her as he took off down the street.

After an hour, Willa Mae declared the mission a failure. Obviously, Ms. Dorn had no intention of sharing the contest rules with her but lacked the spine to say so. Well, there were plenty of other ways to communicate, and Willa Mae intended to investigate all of them.

She started her car, put it in gear, and leaned on her horn as she drove off and didn't let up on it for a good three blocks.

"If you want a fight, sister," she muttered, "you've come to the right place!"

~*~

Odell couldn't get over how easy it had been to connect with Ramona. He didn't consider himself a smooth operator by any stretch of the imagination—his or anyone else's. A widower for several years, Odell just hadn't felt motivated to meet anyone new. This thing with Ramona Dorn, whatever it was, just seemed to have happened. And he couldn't have been happier.

Their late afternoon picnic in the park had been pleasant and surprisingly free of odd or awkward moments. For some reason, he'd felt genuinely comfortable with her. And, as far as he could tell, she felt comfortable, too. Their conversation had been light and chatty, never drifting into serious areas beyond a recognition of their shared status as singles.

He guessed Ramona was about his age—in her mid-forties, give or take a couple years. Attractive and well-spoken, she seemed completely at ease with him being in uniform, something many civilians simply couldn't manage. She had a captivating smile and a self-effacing manner, attributes she shared with his late wife. In short, Ramona was a keeper, assuming she felt the same way about him, and he definitely wanted to find out.

The sun had dropped below the treetops, and their already shady retreat darkened further. "I didn't mean to completely clobber your evening," he said.

"You haven't," she replied. "It's been a while since..." She paused, as if searching for the right words. "Since I've done anything like this, something... spontaneous. Thank you for that."

"So, does that mean you'd be okay with doing it again?" He grinned.

"Have another picnic?"

"Chips and cheese are nice, but I was thinking about something with real food."

"Like what, a cook-out?" Her laugh said more than her words.

"Actually, I'd rather let someone else do the cooking," he said. "There are a couple good restaurants in town."

"I might be talked into something like that," she said. "My social calendar isn't exactly jammed full these days."

"How 'bout tomorrow night?"

She tapped her cheek as she gave the idea some thought. "I could do that, I suppose. Provided...."

"What?" Feeling a great deal less than confident, he tried not to let it show.

"Can you wear something other than your uniform?"

He exhaled in relief. "I think I can scare something up." *Surely, I have some jeans and a golf shirt kickin' around somewhere.* He nodded. "I had no idea you'd be so hard to please."

~*~

Sheila entered the church through a back entrance. The door to the meeting room she'd read about on the internet stood open, and a woman in bright clothing stood beside it, greeting those who entered.

Wearing her best victim look, Sheila nodded at the greeter and passed into the room where the grief-stricken would soon begin their tales of woe. She'd watched similar performances before, and they always struck her as testimonials for weakness. Keeping a neutral expression during the whole thing had always proven difficult, but she managed, mostly by searching the male faces for someone she might approach.

The problem that evening was an utter lack of potential. The few males in the room appeared to have come either from public housing or nursing homes.

She'd wasted her time and left before the meeting ended, pleading another engagement. Having already written off her first effort to find a sugar daddy, she immediately geared up for a different approach. The town of St. Charlotte may not have been a great metropolis, but it had its share of bars and taverns, and that's where she intended to continue her search.

One bar in particular had popped up on her radar the day she arrived. She'd only been there once, and hadn't stayed long, but it seemed to have the sort of clientele she sought. She climbed in her car and headed for an establishment called the Deep Six.

Her previous visit had been during daylight hours. In the growing darkness of early evening, its décor appeared much less generic. Colored lights and illuminated beer signs featuring scantily clad females broke up the prevailing shadows. The smell of old cigarette butts, fresh sweat, and cheap cologne added to the bordello-like ambiance.

Sheila felt right at home.

Sauntering up to the bar, Sheila slid onto a barstool, crossed her legs, and turned slightly to one side, exposing a bit of thigh in the process. Someone once told her the tactic reminded them of baiting a trap. She had no problem with that; she had great legs and was quite proud of them. Besides, the pose gave her as good a look at the customers as they had of her. A win-win.

The male population in the Deep Six definitely outnumbered her competition, and the limited number of females made it easier to spot likely marks.

What she needed was someone with property and the wherewithal to gussy it up enough to claim the garden club prize. Therefore, she figured, her target would likely be middle-aged, probably well-dressed, and drinking alone or with one or two friends. She ordered a Margarita and began her search.

It didn't take long before she felt eyes focusing on her from around the room. She brushed curls from her face, surreptitiously unfastened the top button of her blouse, and casually thrust her surgically enhanced bosom outward. She'd barely begun to work through the salted rim of her first Margarita when a tall, slightly pudgy man approached her.

"You like Margaritas, too?" It was more statement than question. "I don't like the frozen kind, though—"

"Slurpy tumors?" she asked, turning slightly to take better advantage of the limited lighting on her best features.

"What? Oh, yeah. Never heard it called that. 'Brain freeze,' though, that's what I'm familiar with." His eyes drifted

36

from her drink to her chest and back. He finally settled on her face. "I'd offer to buy you one, but you're way ahead of me."

"There's an easy remedy for that," she said and guzzled the contents of her glass. Fortunately, the bar hadn't served one of those ridiculous, drink-all-night jobs where they merely waved the tequila bottle over the glass.

He seemed duly impressed. "Damn!" he said in two distinct syllables. "So, *now* can I buy you one?"

Sheila licked a bit of salt from her lip and smiled. "If you think you can afford it."

"Trust me. That won't be a problem." He grinned, exposing a reasonable set of teeth, not sufficiently perfect to be dentures.

"I wish there were a little more room here at the bar," she said, leaning just enough for their shoulders to make contact.

"Shoot, girl!" he said, growing excited. "I got a table all to myself. Over there." He pointed toward a dark corner. "You go on over; I'll order some more drinks."

"Deal," she said and bussed his cheek with the lightest kiss in her repertoire, inhaling as she did. *Hallelujah! No icky aftershave.*

Once they'd settled in, Sheila thanked him for rescuing her from a lonely evening. It seemed, she told him sadly, that since she'd become single, her luck had turned from lousy to miserable.

"How so?" he asked.

"I lost everything in the divorce. He cleaned out our bank accounts, sold the house out from under me, and took off with some floozy."

He appeared sympathetic. "That's awful."

"And you know what the worst part is? I had to give up my garden. You have no idea how I loved all the plants and shrubs. I had a little spot off to the side where I used to sunbathe." She giggled and took a long pull on her drink. "I prob'ly shouldn't tell you this, seeing as how we just met an' all."

"It's okay. Go ahead and tell me."

She dropped her voice to a whisper and leaned closer to him. "I used to sunbathe in the nude." She clapped her palm to her cheek and rolled her eyes toward the ceiling in what she hoped was a convincing show of girlish timidity.

"Seriously? You lay out in your yard in the all-together?"

"Well, there was a fence around the property, so it wasn't like anyone got scandalized. At least, not that I know of. Nobody ever complained."

He whistled and appraised her even more closely. "I can guaran-damn-tee you I wouldn't have complained."

She gave his upper arm a gentle punch. "Aren't you sweet, uh... Is that crazy, or what? I don't even know your name."

"It's Montgomery," he said. "Folks just call me Monty."

"Sounds British. Are you?"

"Naw. I was born and raised right here in St. Charlotte, but I might've had a limey uncle or two."

"I think I'll call you Marty," she said. "It's more American." She offered to shake his hand which he accepted. "I'm Sheila."

"Nice to meet 'cha. So, about this garden of yours. Did

your husband sunbathe out there, too?"

"What? Oh, gosh no. Never. He— Ya know what? I don't wanna talk about him." She polished off her drink. "Shall we get another?"

He signaled for refills.

"I don't think he ever even looked at my garden," she continued. "It was a prize winner, too. Or would've been, if that jerk hadn't taken advantage of me. I was way too trusting."

"You got a prize for your garden?"

"Absolutely! And I was a shoo-in for this year's contest. Big prize, too. Gotta be worth thousands."

"No!"

"I'm not kidding. I've seen the trophy. Here. Wait. I've got some pictures of it on my phone."

Though he'd been impressed with her before, the photos of the garden club's outrageously gaudy prize impressed him still more. "Those are real gems," she said. "And the metals are gold and silver."

She sighed deeply as she put her phone away. "Not that it matters anymore. I don't have a place, much less a spot for a garden."

"Well, I do," he said. "My house isn't much to look at, but I've got a backyard, and with a little cleaning up and your magic touch, I'll bet you could turn it into somethin' special."

"Do you mean it? Seriously?"

"Of course, I'm serious. And I promise, if you decide to sunbathe out there when it's all done, I won't even peek."

She grinned at him over the rim of her glass. She couldn't quite recall whether it was her fourth or her fifth, but it didn't matter. "Y'know, a little peek prob'ly wouldn't hurt."

"It's too dark to see it now," he began.

She put her hand on his arm. "Would it look better by morning light?"

"I believe it would," he said. "I'm sure of it."

~*~

Though Bubba tried to ignore the comments of the old woman who'd interrogated him about the safety of the garden club trophy, much of what she'd said made sense. If someone truly wanted to snatch the prize, they'd have little trouble breaching the puny safeguards he'd told her about. If pressed, he'd have to admit he'd never actually checked to see if the windows were operable much less locked. He'd since seen to that.

The building hadn't been constructed with the idea of securing anything valuable. The doors and windows met the building codes for general-use commercial establishments. It certainly hadn't been designed as a bank, much less something meant to house goods for sale. The tiny kitchen sported some decent equipment, but nothing exotic. It was a meeting hall, for God's sake! Who'd break into a place like that?

After his talk with his Uncle Odell, it occurred to him that no matter who might steal the dadgum trophy, he'd be the prime suspect. That certainly didn't strike him as fair, but in his heart of hearts, he knew that's the way it would play out. He had two choices: grab the thing himself and move to Bora Bora or some other godforsaken place, or make darn sure no one else grabbed it.

Such heavy thoughts left him determined to remain sober and conscientious, at least until he could find a better place to store the gaudy thing. In the meantime, he resolved to add guard duty to his list of chores. With that in mind, he augmented his stash of personal items at the Grand Hall. This included a change of clothes, additional food, and a shotgun he'd had since his teens. While not the most fearsome of weapons, he'd become fairly proficient with it. He wondered about his ability to draw down on a human being instead of a dove or a squirrel, but figured that was something better left to the heat of the moment.

Bubba used duct tape to mount a flashlight under the barrel of his old Remington 20-guage, flipped the light on, and took the first of what he figured would be hourly patrols.

~*~

By the time Ramona returned home, the sky had gone completely dark, not that she minded. She'd spent a delightful, if utterly unexpected, two hours with Odell Odum. The wine, cheese, crackers, and fruit had been lovely but not nearly as palatable as their conversation. She definitely looked forward to seeing him again.

She waltzed into the house all but whistling a happy tune when she found a note from Donny on the kitchen table. Curious, she picked it up and read the brief message:

> Some lady stopped by to pick up a copy of the rules for the garden club thing. She didn't leave her name.

"Oh, fudge!" Ramona muttered. She'd completely forgotten her promise to share the rules with the leader of the county garden club. A glance at the empty wine bottle on the table morphed into a squint, but she knew the fault was hers; she couldn't blame it on the wine.

She put in a call to Willa Mae Sundee hoping to get back in her good graces by emailing the information or delivering it in person. Unfortunately, there was no answer, and Willa Mae's voice mail was full. Ramona couldn't even leave a message.

Ramona did her best to put the issue out of her mind. She had no desire to let it dampen the mood she'd come home with after her impromptu evening with Odell. Sleep came easily that night.

The following morning, she awoke to a dirge playing on her cell phone, a catty little ringtone she had assigned to the listing for Constance DuBois. A chat with the queen bee of the gossip hive didn't strike her as the best way to start the day. But, she realized, if she didn't respond now, the old witch would just keep calling.

"Good morning, Connie," Ramona said.

"Have you seen the paper today?" Constance asked.

Ramona closed her eyes and shook her head. "Uh, no. Why? Have I been fired?" *Please tell me I've been fired!*

"What? No. Don't be ridiculous. That would never be in the paper anyway. I'm talking about an item on the editorial page."

"What's it about?

"The contest, of course! Someone apparently got to the person who writes these things. They're saying the most awful things about us. You have to do something Immediately!"

"What I have to do, Connie, is get some coffee. If that does the trick, I'll begin to wake up. Then I'll likely take a shower and get dressed." She couldn't remember waking up with a headache, but one was well on its way. "The paper will have to wait."

"I can read it to you," Connie said. "Listen—"

"No! Please. I promise I'll read it myself. I'm pretty certain the world will continue in its present orbit for the time it takes me to get moving this morning."

"But—"

"Thanks for the heads up, but I've got to go."

"Ramona, listen to me. I insist—"

"I have to go, as in... You know. *Go!* I'll call you later." Ramona dropped the phone on her bed and hurried into the bathroom. Though likely only a coincidence, Connie's calls often precipitated a potty break.

Eventually Ramona felt awake enough to investigate the gossip's concerns. She couldn't imagine what the paper might have to say about the garden club, especially when so many extraordinary world events demanded the local paper's in-depth opinions.

Ignoring the headlines, Ramona turned to the editorial section and quickly perused the headlines. The item which had precipitated Constance's hissy fit sat smack in the middle of the page. It couldn't be missed, even if one tried. Ramona swallowed. *Oh Lord, what now?*

Garden Club Snub

The *Chatter* has recently become aware of a policy enacted by one of the area's oldest organizations, the St. Charlotte Garden Club. Their late President, Hildegard Henderson, long regarded as a leading light in this community, established a generous reward for a horticultural contest she introduced shortly before her death. For reasons unknown, the club has chosen to restrict entry in the competition to their membership alone, thus leaving out countless

gardeners, growers, and plant enthusiasts from the surrounding area.

The policy, we're told, may actually be a form of revenge against a rival club which caters to residents outside the St. Charlotte city limits. Historically, the county organization has had significantly more success than the older town club at the annual county fair, the only other contest where the two clubs compete head-to-head.

One is left to wonder if the St. Charlotte gardeners are simply afraid to compete or if they've convinced themselves outsiders are unworthy. Either way, it's a sad day for both the club and the community. It's certainly not the sort of behavior we'd expect of our children, nor is it the sort of tactic that will win any friends in this community. But then, with apologies to poet John Donne, maybe the St. Charlotte club is "an island unto itself."

Ramona realized she'd been holding her breath as she read the article. Where in the world had the newspaper gotten the idea the club had snubbed anyone, let alone people living in cow country? The answer occurred to her all too quickly. It had to be Willa Mae Sundee. The woman was clearly obsessed.

Without wasting another moment, Ramona dragged out her membership roster, determined to call an emergency meeting of the club's Executive Committee. This was composed of the club officers and the chairpersons of the various standing committees, a dozen members in all. Knowing Constance DuBois, Ramona assumed they were already aware of the damning editorial.

Though it consumed the better part of the morning, Ramona reached all of the committee members. The meeting would begin at Noon in the ballroom of the CCCC, the Charles County Conference Center.

~*~

Phase Two of Hildegard Henderson's revised life strategy began shortly after the start of Phase One but called for a very different methodology and a profoundly different goal. She had no desire to compete with Leonard's young paramour, but considering his underworld connections, she couldn't ignore the possibility of being left out in the cold, if not dead.

The discovery that Leonard's success came more from his criminal associates than his local business partners offended her deeply. While she knew he worked with dozens of small businesses in and around the county, she had no idea he had either started or purchased all of them. It hadn't previously occurred to her that a number of competing businesses had come to untimely ends, largely due to fires or fatal accidents, and since these tragedies always seemed to benefit Leonard, she suspected he had arranged them. This revelation left her outraged, and Phase Two would allow her to ultimately set things right.

Making dirty money look clean required a number of steps, and though she had no firsthand knowledge of the transactions required, she quickly learned their general order and function.

Simply put, Leonard received money from his criminal partners which he deposited across the accounts of his local businesses. Later, he would see that payments were made to various "insurance" or "consulting" companies operated by the mob. For handling all these transactions, Leonard earned a percentage of the original funds. This made him a very rich man over a fairly short period of time.

Phase Two began when Leonard told Hildie about his escape plan, the means by which he would eventually disassociate himself from the criminal element so the two of them could enjoy a blissful retirement in tropical anonymity.

Hildie only believed in the first part of his plan. She knew she wouldn't be going anywhere with him.

Chapter Four

"I think women are foolish to pretend they are equal to men; they are far superior and always have been."
– William Golding

Sheila opened one eye, instantly suspicious of her surroundings but not quite awake enough to sort out recent events.

Someone lay beside her on the bed, his breath raspy and interspersed with occasional snorts and whistles. As her eyes adjusted to the dim light, the contents of the room gradually became more distinct, and she pieced together enough remembered bits to solve the mystery.

She'd left the bar with a man. Marty, or Morty. She couldn't remember which. He'd seemed quite interested in her story about the gardening competition and had offered to assist her. He claimed to have a backyard that needed a little work and figured the two of them could whip up something spiffy in no time. He even offered to cover the costs. It sounded great at the time.

Sheila had no doubts about the ability of time and

tequila to put things in soft focus, and she rarely allowed herself to give in to their allure. Clearly, the previous evening had been an exception, and judging from the sounds and smells emanating from her bedmate, an unfortunate one.

Intent on not disturbing the sleeper beside her, Sheila took pains to rise as slowly and silently as possible. She located most of her clothing on the floor beside the bed and carried it out of the room to dress.

Though missing her panties and a shoe, she was unwilling to venture back into the bedroom to find them. Instead, she dressed and still barefoot, hunted up Marty or Morty's wallet, intending to reward herself with the price of replacement footwear.

His driver's license all but jumped out at her, and she glanced at the name printed on it. His real name was Montgomery, and as her alcohol addled brain regained something like full function, she recalled not wanting to venture anywhere with someone called "Monty." That just sounded stuck up. So, she'd changed it. He didn't seem to mind.

Unfortunately, Monty had a grand total of six dollars in his wallet. He'd left it on a table by the front door along with his watch, car keys, change, and a flip phone. She looked at the flip phone with disgust. *It must have been some really potent tequila.*

Hoping for a soft drink to tide her over until she could get home and brush her teeth, Sheila opened the refrigerator in the bungalow's cramped kitchen. The stench from whatever had died inside overwhelmed her, and she staggered away as if punched. Balancing tenuously on one leg she toed the door shut and leaned over the sink to throw up.

Before she could complete the maneuver, something moved among the dirty dishes piled inches from her face. Several somethings, in fact, scrabbling in different directions. That sent her reeling away toward the vile smelling 'fridge.

Holding her hand over her mouth, she staggered to the back door. It opened easily to a small, wooden deck overlooking a junk yard in the making. The remnants of three cars, a fishing boat, and a variety of other mechanical carcasses littered a space punctuated by weeds, ratty shrubs, and dead or dying trees.

Sheila managed to reach the wooden railing before sending the contents of her stomach hurtling over the edge. She remained hunched over the rail until her tummy settled, then eased back and wiped her mouth on her forearm. That gave her time to survey the area which "needed a little work."

You'll pay for this, Monty. Oh, yes. You'll pay.

After gathering his wallet, phone, and keys, Sheila held her breath and reopened the refrigerator. As quickly as she could, she distributed his things in various drawers and inside or behind the rank offerings inside the appliance.

Her purse remained where she'd left it, and a quick check of its contents revealed nothing had gone missing. Pulling out her lipstick, she approached the refrigerator. More like a *regurgitator*, she thought, then scrawled *LOSER!* in big red letters across the front of the appliance. That brought a thin smile to her face as she walked out the door and summoned a taxi to return her to the bar where she'd left her car.

Monty. Ick. What in the world was I thinking?

~*~

Willa Mae smiled as she fixed breakfast for her family.

Her husband owned two franchise auto parts stores plus a feed and grain warehouse. A regular ad buyer in the St. Charlotte *Chatter*, he had no trouble eliciting an emergency editorial on his wife's behalf. He hadn't even bothered to argue with her about it; he knew better.

Though Willa Mae had written the original opinion piece, the editor had been kind enough to correct her spelling and punctuation. He'd even made it sound a bit more highfalutin, which suited her just fine.

Willa Mae imagined the look of dismay on the face of that smarmy Ramona Dunn as she read the damning article. It would be ages before she and her ritzy-ditzy gal pals in the city club lived that down. They'd have to come around and change the rules, if only to save face.

While distributing scrambled eggs and bacon on the plates for her family, she conjured up an image of an angry mob of garden clubbers protesting outside Dorn's front door. They'd demand change!

She decided to let the issue simmer another day or so before she called the woman to find out if her strategic move had been a success. Meanwhile, she had hungry mouths to feed.

~*~

Ramona was only mildly surprised to see twice as many spectators at the meeting as there were executive committee members. St. Charlotte was, after all, a fairly small town, and having a one-woman broadcasting system like Constance DuBois insured that any detail of interest would be immediately shared far and wide. Ramona wondered if the woman should apply to the FCC for a license.

"Thank you all for coming on such short notice,' Ramona began. "I'd like to keep this meeting informal, so—'

"What are you going to do about that dreadful editorial in the *Chatter*?" demanded Constance, who had remained on her feet like a politician caucusing before a vote.

"That's what I hope we'll figure out today," said Ramona.

"Well, here's what I think. First—"

"Thank you, Connie. I look forward to hearing your thoughts on the issue when the committee asks for input. For now, however, I must ask you to take a seat and allow us to begin deliberations."

Though she appeared stricken, Constance closed her mouth and lowered her bulk into one of the folding chairs which Bubba, the harried building manager, had set up as quickly as he could.

The committee members gathered around a table at the head of the room, a few feet away from Hildegard Henderson's monstrous namesake award.

"First off," Ramona said when everyone had taken a seat, "has everyone read the item that appeared in today's paper? If not, there are several copies of the editorial page here on the table. Grab one and read it now, please."

Two committee members did so while the others all began speaking at once. Despite the cacophony, it seemed clear to Ramona there were only two sides to the issue— either the club caved to the open competition challenge or they ignored it. There didn't seem to be any middle ground.

When the volume level reached an uncomfortable level, Ramona banged her gavel on the table until everyone settled down. "I said I wanted to keep this informal," she said. "I didn't intend for it to be a free-for-all."

"But this is slander, isn't it?" asked the club's secretary.

Ramona exhaled heavily. "Technically, it would be libel. Libel is a defamatory statement made in writing. Slander is the same thing only spoken."

"We should sue!" groused Constance, her voice piercing. She stood and added, "They're trying to ruin our reputation."

"Will you please hush, Connie?" Ramona tried to sound stern, something she'd never been particularly good at. "I've tried to be nice, but you're being disruptive. Please keep your thoughts to yourself until we're done."

Constance responded with a mighty "Harrumph" but took her seat anyway.

"Just for the heck of it," Ramona said, "let's see a show of hands. How many of you think we should amend the rules to allow non-members to compete?"

Immediately, a slim majority of the attendee's hands went up, including many in the audience.

"If that's how all of you feel," piped Constance, "then there ought to be an entry fee—a big one. But only non-members should have to pay it."

"Constance, please," Ramona pleaded. "You're not helping."

But the big woman went on, undeterred. "We need to find ourselves a lawyer so we can sue the pants off the newspaper."

Her outburst triggered another round of uncontrolled babbling from every corner of the room.

Once again, Ramona had to bang her gavel on the table to restore order. When they settled down, she continued. "Let's think about what might happen if we do as Connie suggests." She looked around the room to make sure she had everyone's attention.

"If we keep the competition closed, aren't we agreeing with everything that was said in the paper?" She had to raise her hands quickly to thwart another verbal uprising. "Think about it! The paper is basically saying we're so afraid of the club in farm country, we aren't willing to risk our precious trophy."

"It's not just the trophy," said a chorus of younger members whose *ad hoc* leader continued, "What about the, uhm, labor deal. Would that be included, too?"

Ramona shrugged. "I guess so."

The previous speaker responded with, "Then, can I change my vote from 'No' to 'Hell no?'"

The volume produced by a crowd of vocal females hardly shook the walls, but it definitely rattled Ramona's nerves. She let the membership vent for a while before laying on once more with her gavel. "Is there anyone in here who thinks it might be a good idea to open the competition?"

A few scattered hands went up. "I'd like to say something about that," said a petite redhead wearing an apron with a hairdresser's logo on it. "I used to be a member of that rural club. There are some nice people in it, but it seems like they all believe our club gets more publicity, and they don't think it's deserved. That's why they work so hard to win the competition at the County Fair."

Another member stood up beside her. "I think it would be a mistake to limit who can compete. It makes us look selfish. It makes us appear afraid of all the other gardeners. Is that what you all want? To look selfish and afraid?"

There were a few grumbles of dissent but nothing like the previous outbursts.

"I think the committee needs to give this whole thing a closer look. In private," Ramona added. "We'll make a recommendation to the general membership at our next meeting, which is only a few days off. That'll give everyone a chance to cool down and think about all this rationally. Fair enough?"

"Can you put that in the form of a motion?" asked the parliamentarian.

"So moved," said Ramona.

"Second," said a senior member sitting beside the secretary.

Ramona acknowledged her with a nod. "All in favor?"

A chorus of "Ayes" gave her the answer she sought. "Good. Now, I'm going to ask everyone who's not a member of the executive committee to leave the room so we may continue."

"Meeting in secret is a nasty way to conduct business," growled Constance.

"Well then," said Ramona, struggling to keep her voice even, "when you become the club president, you can handle things any way you like. But right now, it's up to me, and this is how we're going to do it. I'll see you at the general membership meeting." She concluded with a smile and a wave, then turned her attention back to the committee.

When the spectators had all departed, Ramona sat back in her chair and tried to relax. Everyone seemed eager to hear what she had to say.

"Well, girls, what do you think?"

~*~

Though tired beyond words after staying up all night

54

guarding the Convention Center, Bubba forced himself the next day to keep a watchful eye on every one of the ladies who attended the special meeting. One could never tell who might be up to no good.

The club president had been apologetic about how many extra people showed up and thanked him profusely for setting up chairs for everyone on such short notice. He had been prepared to give the woman grief about it, but she seemed genuinely sincere, an attitude to which he was unaccustomed. It felt nice to be needed.

It felt even better, however, when they left.

The Kiwanis wouldn't be meeting until the following day, so Bubba had plenty of time to get the space ready for them. Besides, he liked the Kiwanians; they often provided a lunch for him if the town's lone caterer prepared enough extra.

He wandered into his office and looked longingly at the sofa. Very little furniture remained useable after the fire destroyed the motel rooms. The sofa had come out of the last room, one which wasn't completely burned up. Though it still bore a mild odor of smoke, Bubba managed to ignore it, especially when he worked himself to a frazzle.

Pulling out the hide-a-bed didn't present too great an obstacle though he had to push his desk out of the way to do it. As he weighed the alternatives of curling up on the sofa or opening it to its full width, he heard a car pull up outside.

Assuming one of the ladies had left something behind, he got up to let her in. The occupant of the car, however, turned out to be someone he'd never seen before. And while he looked vaguely familiar, Bubba decided he couldn't take any chances. So, he went back to his office to retrieve the shotgun.

"The meeting wasn't a total disaster," Ramona said. "We made a few decisions and then went back and forth because no one was happy about any of it."

Odell listened patiently, all the while thinking how happy he was not to be stuck in the middle of it like his dinner companion. "Okay, let me see if I've got this right. The newspaper called out the club for not opening up the contest to the world."

Ramona nodded. "And everyone agreed; that one editorial totally trashed our reputation." She blinked at him. "Who would have ever thought a garden club would need to worry about its reputation?"

Odell chuckled. "You've got a point." After a pause, he added, "And I've gotta say, you have some astonishing points."

"*Excuse me?*"

"You look gorgeous," he said.

"Oh!" She grinned. "I thought— Never mind. Thank you! You look pretty hot yourself, even without your trooper hat and sidearm."

"Can I be honest?"

"That's usually a safe bet," she said.

"I feel sort of undressed without all the gear hangin' off my belt."

She reached out and patted his hand. "I appreciate your sacrifice."

"You're sweet," he said, then cleared his throat. "Prior to this evening, I had no idea you were involved in the garden club."

Ramona inhaled sharply. "That's not a problem, is it? I mean, I can quit. I just need to—"

He gave his head a quick shake. "Don't be silly. I love that you're a gardener. I'm a huge fan of fresh veggies."

"I do flowers. Mostly easy ones."

Oops! Time to backpedal. "I like flowers, too. Really, I do."

"I'm relieved," she said, though she appeared dubious.

"The thing is, I don't know anything about your club except that its last president went missing. How well did you know Mrs. Henderson?"

"I didn't know Hildie very well at all to tell the truth. Ya see, I kinda got snookered into taking the Vice President job, and Hildie was extremely nice to me, tried to make me feel like I could handle things, maybe even make some changes for the better. And then, all of a sudden, she was gone, and I was left in charge. Why do you ask?"

"We got a call from the Feds saying someone tried to use Mrs. Henderson's passport to enter the country."

Ramona looked surprised, but pleased. "Really? You mean she might be okay?"

"We don't know anything for sure. There should have been a surveillance video, but for some reason it's not available." He exhaled in exasperation. "It seems odd to me that she could be alive and not try to contact anyone to let them know. Her husband, at the very least. We reached out to him, but he said he hadn't heard a thing from her since the day she left. I got the impression there was some tension between them."

"I didn't sense anything like that," Ramona said.

"Interesting. It's probably nothing, but if I hear anything else, I'll let you know. I promise."

"Thanks. I'm sure I'm not the only one who's concerned about her."

"Now," he said, hoping to get back on more comfortable ground, "let's get back to your contest dilemma. Did y'all decide to open the competition?"

"Well," Ramona said, "not exactly. I mean, some of the girls were okay with it, but quite a few were against it. The only thing we all agreed on was the need to restore the club's standing in the community."

"And how do you propose to do that?" he asked.

"Well, that's where things pretty much fell apart. We couldn't come up with an idea, much less a plan. I hate to say it, but I'm stumped."

Just then their salads arrived, and they set about the business of eating. Odell welcomed the extra time it afforded him to try and think of a solution for the gardeners. Meanwhile, Ramona appeared to be dissecting her salad, carefully extracting certain elements with surgical precision.

He pointed at her salad with his fork. "What in the world are you doing?"

"There's something about the tomatoes," she said. "They taste a little funny."

Odell stared down at his own salad. "You think they're spoiled or something?"

"It's nothing that dramatic. It's just— I dunno. They look red but taste green, and it seems like the flavor competes with the lettuce."

He thought about that for a moment and then smiled.

"That might be your answer."

"What? *Tomatoes?*"

"No. Competition."

She looked at him as if he were sprouting a second nose, somewhere near the middle of this forehead.

"I don't think you should give in to the newspaper or the other club. What if we came up with some sort of oddball competition, something the public would want to watch? The winner would get to decide if the garden club contest is open or not. That way, both sides would be assured of working hard to win."

Ramona squinted at him. "I don't get it. Why would our club bother to compete? We already have the right to say no."

"True. But if you do, your club's going to look chicken. You'd likely have to endure jokes and snickers behind your back. You don't want that, and based on what you told me about the committee, they don't want that either. What you need is a way to save face without being forced to give in."

Still not fully convinced, she urged him to go on.

"What if you found a really deserving charity and staged some sort of contest between your club and the rural outfit? All proceeds would go to the charity. You could even play it up as a grudge match. Winner takes all, even though the real winner is the charity, no matter which side scores the most points."

Ramona eased back in her seat as their main course arrived. Reaching a conclusion on Odell's idea didn't take long. "Y'know. The more I think about it, the more I like the idea. So, have you got any ideas about what kind of contest it could be? There are a ton of different charities we could support. I guess we could decide on that later."

"I'm sure you could find some way to compete, but I think it'd have to be athletic. It has to be something intriguing. Maybe softball, flag football... Bowling?" He started laughing.

"What's so funny?"

"If you really wanted to draw a crowd, you could do it in the buff."

"*In the nude?*" The color drained from Ramona's face.

"Of course, I'd have to arrest everybody for public indecency, but that could wait 'til half-time or somewhere in the fifth inning."

"You can't be serious!"

He kept laughing. "Of course not, but still...."

"Still what?" She looked anything but amused.

"It would definitely draw a crowd."

"Have you always been such a male chauvinist pig, or is this something new?"

He frowned, theatrically. "It's never a good idea to call a cop a pig."

"Different species."

"Doesn't matter."

"Look," he said, finally able to keep a straight face. "This is really a two-part deal. First, you've got to find the right charity, something that will appeal to just about everyone. It probably oughta have something to do with kids. Sick or injured kids, most likely. Then, you've got to find something competitive that's fun to watch. Doesn't really matter what it is—pie-eating, a showdown with paintball guns, whatever. Make it appealing enough, and in support of a deserving charity, and folks will come out and pay to watch you. Telling them it's the fight of the century would only make it more interesting."

Ramona smiled as she started eating her dinner, which fortunately hadn't completely cooled off. "I don't know if you're a genius or a tease."

"Can't I be both?"

She shook her head. "I don't think that's allowed."

He shrugged. "I'll settle for genius."

"That's kinda what I'm thinking," she said. "I've gotta run this by the committee, but I've got a sneaking suspicion they'll like the idea."

"Good," said Odell. "Another fire doused. I should probably get an award of some kind."

"Flower of the month?"

"Spare me. *And* the poor flowers. They come to my house to die. Horribly."

It became her turn to chuckle. "I could fix that."

He stared into her beautiful eyes. "I'll just bet you could."

~*~

Hildegard Henderson had looked forward to Phase Three of her plan for quite some time. Phase One would continue indefinitely because she so enjoyed looking and feeling physically fit. She had even garnered a provocative glance or two from Ramona's son, Donny, when they were discussing the landscape service portion of the contest award. She hadn't gone out of her way to flaunt her improved figure and appearance, but she certainly enjoyed his positive reaction. She would reward herself as soon as the next part of the plan was complete.

She had wrapped up Phase Two with the development of her namesake gardening competition and the Trust she'd established to keep it going. Leonard had played along as she hoped he would, picking up the tab for the ghastly trophy. He hadn't realized how she'd funded the Trust or more importantly, her very own escape plan, and that marked the start of Phase Three. She needed to be well away from St. Charlotte when he found out.

The fact he had no clue what she was up to made her all but giddy. She understood how he remained oblivious to her physical changes, since they hadn't made love in a long time, and she had done her best to disguise the improvements she'd achieved in her physique. The better she looked, the less she cared about him.

Phase Three called for travel, and as she had anticipated, Leonard was far too busy to accompany her.

Chapter Five

"If you want something said, ask a man. If you want something done, ask a woman." – Margaret Thatcher

Sheila hurried back to her room at the extended stay motel as quickly as she could. While visions of nasty, crawly things and vile smells occupied her mind, she focused on the one option that might provide her with some measure of relief: a shower. The hotter, the better.

With the door closed and locked behind her, she disrobed while racing to the bathroom barely avoiding a fall in the process. She couldn't get the curtain closed nor the hot water on fast enough but eventually stood under a scalding, pulsing stream of liquid resurrection. The sooner she could bathe away traces of her tryst, the better.

She washed her hair with something approaching zeal and scrubbed every exposed skin cell, including those in the spaces between her toes. Then she rinsed herself until she exhausted the hot water supply.

Though refreshed and clean, at last, she still berated herself for not recognizing Monty for the rat he turned out to be. She had to be more careful; the prize was too important to leave to chance. While she might have felt comfortable in a bar as sleazy as the Deep Six, it certainly wasn't the hunting ground she needed to find the perfect target.

She had to find a man with both cash and class, someone willing to do what she needed done in order to maintain a relationship with her. And it would help mightily if that someone had at least a smattering acquaintance with the St. Charlotte Garden Club.

Sheila thought back to the newspaper article about the upcoming contest which initially sparked her interest and drew her to the south Georgia town. Where had she put the darned thing? That thought sparked a brief but furious search ending with a carefully folded page of newsprint.

She reviewed the story about the contest and its namesake, Hildegard Henderson, wife of Leonard Henderson, who owned many small businesses in and around St. Charlotte. Hildegard had disappeared under mysterious circumstances and was presumed dead. According to the printed account, Leonard had been devastated by the news.

That all happened months earlier. Sheila's history with wealthy men suggested they tended to recover more quickly than their female counterparts. If that held true for Leonard Henderson, now might be a great time to get acquainted.

If only she could figure out where and how to approach him.

~*~

Disappointed by the lack of response after the *Chatter's* editorial shaming the city garden club, Willa Mae Sundee felt like snarling at the whole world. She'd been certain the hit piece would've rocked the little world of the

"Saint Charlatans." And yet she hadn't heard a peep out of them. Her husband had checked with the paper's editor who claimed he hadn't heard a word of protest, much less rancor, when that sort of thing was rarely delayed.

What were they up to?

Though she felt sure she had never met Ramona Dorn, she had no trouble conjuring a mental image of her. Willa Mae had become adept at such imaginings after being forced to spend considerable time by herself since her husband's companies kept him constantly engaged elsewhere. And, having grown up in an even more rural part of the state, Willa Mae's childhood had been solitary save for a sprinkling of proverb-spouting adults.

She thus leaned on counsel gleaned from older sources, like her dear old Aunt Hattie. The occasion had become enshrined in Willa Mae's memory to be trotted out as needed when counseling her own children or those simply in need of such wisdom.

Though dentally challenged, Aunt Hattie typically smiled as she dispensed advice, especially when working with a toddler learning the skills needed to successfully navigate a modern flush toilet. The aged matron, a product of the deep, deep South, held proper etiquette above all else.

"Five squares is all ya need," she would say, carefully counting out and folding thin sheets of toilet tissue into layers. "In this whole world, there's only two kinds of people: them that folds the tissues, and them that just wads 'em all up. And, missy, you kin tell which is which just by lookin' at 'em."

Having held the truism close to her heart, Willa Mae instinctively concluded that Ramona Dorn had to be a wadder. She knew it automatically, not even needing a glance at the Charlatan's presiding officer.

Content with her conclusion and with a comfortingly smug smile, Willa Mae gave thought to her options regarding the contest and what she might do to add additional pressure to the city club's leadership. It had to be public, whatever it was, and it had to be specific. There would be no point in leaving it up to anyone's interpretation.

She put in a call to her husband's office.

"I'm sorry, Miz Sundee, but your husband isn't in right now. I think he—"

Willa Mae instantly recognized the voice of Robert's secretary. "That's okay, Darla, I called to talk to Wyatt. Is he in?"

Wyatt handled all the advertising for the firm and designed the ads they ran in the *Chatter* and papers in nearby towns where Willa Mae's husband had dealerships. She was quickly connected to the pleasant young man.

"Hey, Miz Sundee. You doin' all right?"

"As always," she said. "Listen, I need your help. Can you whip up a few little signs for me? I need 'em about the size of a sheet of typing paper."

"No problem. If a black and white message will do, I can crank 'em out pretty quick. Color might take a bit longer."

She discussed the details and got his input on the best way to phrase her message. After thanking him, she hung up and glanced at the clock. He'd have them ready by lunchtime, which gave her all afternoon to distribute them to every nursery and plant vendor in the area.

If Ramona didn't get the message, her fellow club members certainly would.

~*~

Bubba didn't recognize the car parked just outside the building, nor did he know the driver. Not usually intimidated by men taller or heavier than he was, Bubba realized he needed to protect more than himself. He'd been entrusted with the safety of the garden club's prize.

Swallowing, he stood the shotgun on the floor, barrel up and within easy reach. He'd already pumped a round into the chamber. If the visitor wanted trouble, Bubba was quite ready to deliver it.

He didn't wait for the caller to knock on the door. Instead, he opened it, tried to smile, and said, "The meeting hall's closed. Won't be in use again 'til tomorrow."

"That's okay," said the visitor, a man who stood a good bit taller than Bubba. "I came to see the big deal trophy my girlfriend told me about last night."

"Sorry," Bubba said, "Can't let anyone in who isn't part of an organization that rents the hall. And then only for set-up and cleanup outside the meeting hours." He shrugged. "Rules is rules. I don't make 'em, but I hafta enforce 'em."

"C'mon, man. I just wanna take a quick look. Won't take ten seconds."

Bubba just shook his head while he reached for the shotgun.

"Listen, pal. Think of this as a mission of mercy. My girlfriend is all about this stupid prize. She couldn't stop talkin' about it last night, I swear. I just wanted to see what she was goin' on about. Who knows? Maybe I could have a replica made for her. The thing is, I'm losing her, and I've gotta do something, something big."

The guy sounded sincere, but Bubba knew he had no

business claiming he could read anyone's character unless they wore it like a tattoo on their forehead.

"I'll make it worth your while," the visitor said. "How's ten bucks sound?"

Bubba huffed. "I'm not about to lose my job over a lousy ten dollars. Make it fifty."

The offer stunned the visitor. "*Fifty?* For just a look-see? That don't seem fair. How 'bout twenty?"

"Why should I? Man, I don't even know your name," Bubba said.

His visitor stuck out his hand. "It's Montgomery. You can call me Monty."

Bubba quickly did some math. Twenty bucks would keep him in beer all weekend. After shaking hands, he picked up the shotgun and backed away, waving Monty in.

Monty's eyes went wide when he saw the Remington in his host's hands. "Holy moly, dude! What's with the cannon?"

"It's insurance. You can set the money on my desk over there, and we'll head into the hall where the trophy is."

Monty pulled out his wallet and produced a five and a single. "Well, just damn. Seems I'm a little short. Can I owe ya?"

Already regretting his decision to let the man in, Bubba exhaled in exasperation. "Nah. Just forget it. Leave what you've got there, then head on through that door." He gestured with the shotgun.

"Fine," said Monty as he complied. "But would you mind pointin' that thing at the floor? I'd hate for you to trip and blow my head off."

"No problem," Bubba said. "I'll just point it at your butt. If it goes off, you can get by with one cheek." He smiled thinking he'd come up with a brilliantly half-assed solution.

Monty muttered as they entered the hall. Bubba couldn't make out his words but guessed that was just as well. They came to a halt next to the gaudy prize, and Monty whistled.

"Well, that's somethin' all right. You got any idea what it's worth?"

Bubba shook his head. "All I know is it's heavy as all git out. I had to bring it in and put it on that stand. Thought I'd throw my back out."

It was Monty's turn to shake his head. "When is this contest, anyway? Has it started yet?"

"Durned if I know," Bubba said. "But I can tell you one thing for sure: I'm ready for it to be over."

~*~

"So," Ramona said at a second emergency meeting of her club's executive committee, "I think I've got a way to get us out of this ugly situation." That comment garnered the attention of every member of the group.

"As some of you know, I live on the outskirts of town, not far from Planter's Park. In fact, I was impressed by some of the signs our club put in that park to identify interesting native plants and flowers; it's one of the reasons I joined."

"Presumably there's a point to this preamble," said the secretary. "I'm not sure how much of this I need to record."

"None of it, yet, Marlie. Just bear with me." Ramona smiled with more confidence than she'd felt since the day Hildie had gone missing. "As I walked by the park this afternoon, I saw a young boy and his mother standing near the playground. The boy wore braces on his legs and supported himself with the kind of crutches that fit around his upper arms."

"My nephew's child has cerebral palsy and needs that kinda stuff in order to get around," said the chair of the hospitality committee. "The poor kid has a heck of a time just walking down the hall."

"Can he use a normal playground?" Ramona asked.

The committee members exchanged blank looks. "Well, sure. Why not?" asked the head of the membership committee. "I mean, he wouldn't be excluded, would he?" She squinted. "Is this an insurance issue or a civil rights thing?"

"It's neither," Ramona assured her. "The fact is, there's not a single playground in this entire county that's designed with handicapped children in mind. That kid with the crutches? He can't use any of the normal playground equipment, no slides, no swing sets, no climbing structures, nothing."

"Where are you going with this, Ramona?" asked Marlie.

"Great question! And it just might be the answer to our contest dilemma. What if we challenged the county club to some sort of competitive event and used the proceeds to create a playground for kids with special needs?"

The head of the yearbook committee looked dubious "We're a garden club. Why would we build a playground?"

"Because nobody else has," Ramona said. "Think of the great publicity we'd get. And it's an idea everyone would support. We could do some lovely plantings there, too. Something for the adults to enjoy while their children play. C'mon, who doesn't love kids, especially kids who have problems they didn't create?"

"Okay, I get that," said the chair of the heirloom plants committee. "But why would the country gardeners agree to help, especially when we just snubbed them over the Hildie Henderson contest?"

"Because we'd offer to open up the contest to them if they can beat us in whatever game or contest we use to support the charity. They get to help a great cause *and* have a chance to get what they want. We win either way, because we'll have done something for the community."

The group went silent for several beats, then everyone began talking at once. Ramona still hadn't gotten used to it.

"Hold on now," said Marlie. "I'm taking notes as fast as I can. You're saying if we lose this charity competition, whatever it is, we'll have to open Hildie's contest to the whole world, or just the club out in the boondocks?"

"The whole world," Ramona said. "And why not? The rules say the winner has to return the trophy to the club for the next year's event. The winner could belong to any garden club anywhere, or no garden club at all."

"I don't like it," said the heirloom gardener, a tall, thin woman with a shock of white hair. "A competitor ought to at least have a sponsoring organization, shouldn't she?"

Marlie chimed in, "Is this thing only for women? I mean, there's a whole bunch of men who love gardening. Like my husband for instance. Why should he be left out?"

"Men shouldn't be excluded," Ramona said, trying to gauge the group's direction. "Let's take an informal vote. How many of you like the general idea?"

"Of letting men enter the big contest?"

"No, of the whole thing—the charity event and the possible opening of Hildie's contest to the world."

Marlie counted the yes votes, and only two members didn't raise their hands. "Looks like you've got some support," she said.

"So, all we need now is an excuse for the challenge. We've got a couple really good golfers in the club," said the membership chair. "We could stage a tournament."

Ramona held up her hands. "Let's not get ahead of ourselves. I'm guessing the rural club would be much more inclined to go along with us if they have a say in the event. I suggest we delegate two or three people to meet with two or three of the other club's leadership to work out the details."

The suggestion was greeted with some grumbling, but most went along with the idea. "Since I came up with this plan, I'll be happy to do my part," Ramona said. "Who'd like to go with me?"

~*~

Sheila agreed with what many con artists had proven time and again; rich widowers were valuable marks, though not always easy ones. A successful con required careful planning and a studied approach. It wouldn't do to look up Leonard Henderson in the phone book and show up on his doorstep with some lame tale of woe. Successful businessmen rarely got that way by being stupid, and she felt sure her target would not be an exception. Job number one, therefore, had to be reconnaissance. Once she knew the places he went and the things he did—his haunts and habits—she'd have a much better line on how to approach him.

It all boiled down to a simple case of stalking.

Gathering the necessary supplies became the first step. She'd have to load everything into her car and be ready to conduct an extended surveillance. At some point she might even want to bug his home or office, something she'd done before and felt comfortable doing again. The Internet made it easy to get any of the gadgetry she might need, provided she didn't go broke first.

"Oh, Leonard dear, you have no idea what awaits you," she said as she piled an armload of provisions in the back seat of her car. "No idea at all."

~*~

Surprised by how many miles she'd driven, Willa Mae left the last nursery on her list and headed for home. Though tired, she was satisfied by her efforts, and it seemed all the plant sellers in the county felt the same way. After all, the more people competing for the city club's prize, the more products they stood to sell.

Still, it puzzled her why the Charlatans insisted on keeping the contest all to themselves. She only knew one person who belonged to that club, but she'd been reluctant to call her and get the inside scoop. It wouldn't have been an issue except the woman had once dated Willa Mae's husband, Bob. Doubtless, he couldn't have cared less if the two women had a conversation, as long as it wasn't about him.

Gritting her teeth, Willa Mae figured she could go through with it provided the information proved useful. That seemed like a big "if," but what alternative did she have? While on the way home, she dialed the woman's number and waited for the call to be answered.

"Marlie? Hey! This is Willa Mae Sundee. I hope I didn't catch you at a bad time."

"Willa? My gosh, I haven't heard from you in forever."

"That's my fault," Willa Mae said, trying not to bite her tongue. "I should've done a better job keeping in touch."

"So, how's Robbie?"

"Bob's fine, thank you." *Robbie?* She hadn't heard that name in years. She quickly suppressed thoughts of her husband as a young man with his arms around Marlie Sorenson, varsity cheerleader and star of the high school tennis team. "So, I was hoping you could clear up a little something for me."

"I can try."

"You're in the St. Charlotte garden club, aren't you?"

"I'm the secretary."

Oh? Interesting. "I read something in the paper and wondered—"

"You saw that editorial? Wasn't it awful? They smeared us! Made us sound so... I don't know, petty. It wasn't right, especially after everything we've done for this town over the years. I'm thinking about dropping my subscription."

"I don't blame you," Willa Mae said. "I imagine your club's pretty upset."

"Some are; some aren't. You know how it is."

"So, what's the big deal? Why not open the contest? I mean, I haven't seen the trophy up close, but I saw a picture of it in the paper. And, well, I'm no art collector, but you've gotta admit, it's not exactly a thing of beauty."

Marlie paused. "I probably shouldn't say this...."

"Say what? You can trust me."

"It's a two-part prize."

"There's a cash award, too?" *Ha! No wonder Ramona Dorn wouldn't share the details!*

"No," said Marlie. "It's...."

"It's what?"

74

"In addition to the trophy, the winner gets free landscaping services from a local provider—one week a month for a whole year."

Oh. "Well, that's something. Pretty generous, too. Do you know which company they'll use?"

"Designs by Donny, I think."

"Never heard of 'em. But why would you be reluctant to tell me about it?"

"I'm getting there," Marlie said, "But this part has got to stay between you and me. You swear?"

Intrigued, Willa Mae pulled off the road to concentrate. "I do! Honest. I won't tell a soul. Go on!"

"I don't know this first-hand of course. I'm just passing along what I've heard."

"Sure, sure. Go on."

"It's not the landscaping that's got so many of the younger club members' attention. It's the land-*scapers.*"

"I don't get it."

"I'm told they're all striking young guys. They strut around in shorts with their shirts off. I think it's disgusting, personally, as do most of the older members, but a few of the girls think it's... well, sexy."

"Isn't there a nightclub in Atlanta or Savannah where those ladies can see guys with their clothes off?" Willa Mae asked.

"I suppose," said Marlie. "But there aren't any places like that around here. And these guys bring the show right to the back yard."

"Hm."

"I've heard the shows sometimes go on *indoors*."

"*No!*"

"Yes!" Marlie giggled. "But you've gotta swear you didn't hear that from me."

"I won't breathe a word of it to anyone," Willa Mae said. "I promise."

"I'd love to chat more, but I've gotta go," Marlie said. "Give my regards to Robbie."

"It's Bob."

"Right."

~*~

Ramona told herself the Executive Committee meeting hadn't been a complete disaster. At least they agreed on Odell's suggestion about connecting the gardening contest to a charitable event. How could they not?

Sadly, not a single soul offered to serve on a tiny, short-term committee to work out a deal of some kind with their rural counterpart. When no one volunteered, Ramona contemplated an effort to shame them into it, then gave up. Most of the senior members, those who'd been part of the club for a decade or more, declined on the grounds they'd already put in enough time and effort on the club's behalf. They urged her to recruit some of the younger members.

What they wouldn't acknowledge was the fact that many of the younger members were still working full-time or had children and family commitments that prevented more active participation. Gardening, it seemed, was the kind of pastime folks pursued when and as they could.

Ramona gave some thought to pouring herself a glass of wine and/or taking a nap. Maybe one first, and then the other. But she knew it was still too early in the day, and what if Donny came home before he usually did? He might think she was turning into a lush.

Ultimately, she skipped the wine and settled for a nap. With any luck, she'd have a dream about Odell.

~*~

Hildegard knew she had little time to prepare for her escape; it had to happen before Leonard discovered what she had done to fund her long-term getaway. She told him she'd been asked by friends to take a cruise to the Holy Land, something she claimed she'd always wanted to do.

He seemed surprised by the suddenness of it, but acquiesced when she asked if he objected and declined, as she knew he would, when she asked him to come with her.

"Are you sure you don't want to come along? This last-minute deal is amazing; it would be a shame to miss out on it."

"I'm sure you're right," he said, "but I've got some business to attend to in Atlanta. I won't be back before you leave."

She managed a frown despite harboring no shred of sadness. The sort of business he handled in Atlanta was female and young enough to be his daughter. The Hendersons had graduated from separate beds to separate bedrooms years before. That, coupled with the underworld career he'd jumped into, left her uncaring.

"Well, that's disappointing," she said, "but you know your business. You've got a day or so to change your mind."

With Leonard off to a rendezvous with his girlfriend, Hildie set about preparing for her own travels. She packed two roll-around suitcases and one large, reinforced cardboard box. The luggage contained clothing and travel items, the box held just over two hundred thousand dollars in cash which she'd taken from Leonard's short-term stash, bulk currency he'd received from his gangster pals but not yet processed. He wouldn't discover the substantial shortage until well after she'd gone. How he explained it to the mob was his problem.

She packed the smaller of the two rolling bags in a cardboard box along with the cash and mailed it to a postal box she'd rented from a service company near the Atlanta airport, the only one which offered large enough storage space. With the rest of her escape plans fully realized, she took a taxi to the church where she met with the group headed for the Holy Land, a destination she would never reach.

Chapter Six

"If you want something said, ask a man. If you want something done, ask a woman." – Margaret Thatcher

Sheila had spent several hours in her car on a shady street opposite Leonard Henderson's stately home. Late afternoon had come and gone when his garage door finally rolled up, and Leonard rolled out.

Following him proved almost too simple; the man obeyed every traffic sign and speed limit as he made his way toward the interstate highway and headed for Atlanta.

Sheila checked her gas gauge, relieved to see slightly over a half tank. That would be enough to get her to the city and back, assuming Leonard didn't do too much sightseeing. Fortunately, her target had timed his drive appropriately and missed the worst of the city's horrendous rush-hour traffic. She kept a car or two in between their vehicles as she followed doggedly behind him.

When he pulled up to the front of an upscale apartment building, she found a spot in the parking lot which gave her a good view as he exited his car and stood waiting by the passenger door. Within moments, an attractive young woman flounced out of the building and approached him with all the zest of a teenaged cheerleader. The two embraced, and Leonard guided her into the car, resumed his spot behind the wheel, and drove off.

Sheila, still stunned by the sheer youth and seductiveness of the other woman, had to force herself to pursue them. She doubted the need for stealth as Leonard seemed far too engaged with his passenger to note whether or not someone might be following him. As a result, she pulled in right behind him and followed all the way to the sculpted grounds and dramatically illuminated Le Grande restaurant, often called the most exclusive watering hole in the Southeast.

Leonard handed his car keys to a valet and strolled arm-in-arm with his young companion to the entrance where a liveried doorman greeted them like old friends. Leonard ushered the femme fatale ahead of him and administered a slight pinch to her bottom as she passed in front of him. The little idiot giggled in response.

Sheila felt ill. Her efforts had been wasted. Leonard Henderson may as well have been guarded by a phalanx of palace guards. She'd never get as close to him as she needed to, not with such a sweet young thing already hanging on his arm.

Muttering and cursing her luck, Sheila turned her car around and headed back to St. Charlotte. Tired and disillusioned, she pulled to a stop in the lot beside the Deep Six, grabbed her purse, and marched inside.

~*~

"Donny?"

"Hey, Momma. I just got home." Donny kept his

distance. "I need a shower pretty bad."

Ramona caught the proof of his statement without going near him. "Sure, hon. But first, a quick question."

"Shoot."

"I'm curious about the arrangement you made with Hildie Henderson."

He chuckled. "Best deal I ever made. Guaranteed income."

"How does that work, exactly?"

"Whoever wins tells me what they want done. I send a crew to handle the job, and I send a bill to the trust."

"You've got more than one crew?" Ramona asked.

"I've got two."

"And which crew do you work with?"

He shrugged. "It depends on the job. Usually I go with the diggers."

"Diggers?" Ramona squinted at him.

"Yeah. They do the hard stuff. The other crew is made up of guys I knew in school." He lifted his arm, sniffed, and rolled his eyes toward the ceiling. "Oh, man. I *really* need a shower."

Her cell phone rang, as it had for much of the afternoon. She nodded at her son. "Yeah, fine. Go," she said as she answered the phone.

"Is this Ramona Dorn, president of the St. Charlotte Garden Club?"

"It is."

"I'd like some information about the big contest y'all

are runnin'."

Ramona shook her head. *Where were all these calls coming from?* "We haven't completely formalized everything just yet, but I'll be happy to take your name and address and mail you a copy of the rules as soon as we've worked out all the details."

"That'd be just fine. I'm so happy the contest is open to the public."

"Actually, that's one of the details we haven't worked out just yet."

"That's odd. Thing is, I was over at Wolf's Nursery a while ago. You know Don Wolf, don't ya? Nice man. Great with the ladies, but I think it's his wife who's the plant expert. I think he just follows orders. Anyway, that's where I saw the sign."

"Sign?" Ramona asked. "What sign?"

"The one about your contest. It said we should call and make arrangements to enter. Had your name and number on it."

Ramona jotted down the caller's information and promised to let her know when the club finalized the rules. She then called Karla Boyd, a long-time club member who handled the club's newsletter and publicity.

"You didn't happen to put out a flyer about our contest, did you?"

"Flyer? Was I supposed to put out a flyer? Nobody told me about any flyers! Is it too late? Is there anything—"

"Relax, Karla," Ramona said, trying to sound reassuring. "It seems someone is distributing notices to all the garden shops and nurseries telling people to call me about the contest. I thought maybe you knew something about it."

"I'm glad to hear that," Karla said.

"You're *glad* someone's putting out unauthorized notices?"

"No, of course not. I'm just glad it wasn't something I was *supposed* to do. I've got my hands full getting the newsletter ready every month. You know how some of the senior gals are; they want printed copies of *The Blossom*. None of that new-fangled email stuff for them! But oh, what a pain in the rear it is for me. And time-consuming. The cost of ink for my poor printer. Oh, and the postage—"

"I completely understand," Ramona said, hoping to calm her down. Karla was usually a voice of reason she could count on. She had no intention of alienating her. "I'd just like to get a handle on this. I can't imagine who would deliberately stir things up."

"Hold on a sec, will you?" Karla asked. "I need a little more wine."

Ramona glanced at the clock, relieved to note it was a little past five, the beginning of what a friend referred to as the "Adult Beverage Hour."

"Okay, I'm back," Karla said. "Know what? I bet whoever did those signs is the same person who got the *Chatter* to run that nasty editorial. That's what I think. What do you need me to do?"

"Just keep your ears open." Ramona sighed. "Now I know how the White House feels when they suspect someone on the inside is leaking information."

"Let's hope it's not that serious," Karla said.

"No kidding. I'll catch you later."

Ramona set her phone down, retrieved a wine glass from the cabinet, and was ready to serve herself when the phone rang yet again.

"Hello?" she said, unable to keep the irritation from her voice.

"Whoa," said Odell. "Sounds like I got you at a bad time."

The man's voice triggered a wave of relief. "I'm sorry. I didn't mean to come off like such a... I dunno. Stinker."

He laughed. "No worries."

"What's up?"

"I think I might have a solution for your competition dilemma."

"Really? What is it?"

"Here's the thing. I'm afraid if I just tell you about it, you'll make up your mind without really giving it a chance."

Ramona stared at her cell phone as if she might be able to see Odell's face and try to read it. "Uh, okay. So how else am I going to find out what this mysterious solution is?"

"Come with me tonight and see a demonstration."

"*Tonight?*"

"Yeah. And we'll need to hurry. It requires a bit of a drive, and I don't want to be late. We need to see it from the very beginning."

Though definitely intrigued, Ramona needed a little more to go on. "Where are we going? And do I need to dress up?"

"Atlanta. And casual is fine. I'm wearing jeans."

"And a holster?"

"Nah." He chuckled. "Not even a badge. This is just for fun. For me, anyway. For you, it's more like scouting a professional venue. I've even lined up an interpreter."

"Seriously? This thing, whatever it may be, is in a foreign language?"

"Sorta," he said. "But you'll just have to wait and see for yourself."

Ramona couldn't imagine what he had in mind. "Are you sure this is on the level?"

"I'm a cop, darlin'. It's absolutely on the level."

"Not all cops are honest."

"This one is," he said. "You in, or not?"

The decision couldn't have been easier. "Of course, I'm in!"

"Good. 'Cause I'm parked outside your house. You've got exactly two minutes to jump in the car with me."

"But—"

"Make that a minute and fifty-eight seconds."

~*~

Bubba was only too happy to get away from the Convention Center where he'd been stuck since the Kiwanis luncheon ended. He finally got a break when the Jaycees arrived for their monthly get-together. Since beer and barbecue were the order of the day, Bubba knew he'd have several hours to himself.

Once free of the relentlessly boring confines of the CCCC, he instinctively headed to his favorite watering hole where he settled into an open seat at the bar. The lights were dim, as usual, and though a few people danced to a tune on the juke box, most of the patrons occupied booths. A quick scan of the interior told him he was the only customer without one or more companions.

"Hey there, Bubba," said Wanda Pritchett, the owner, operator, and principal bartender of the Deep Six. "What can I getcha?"

"I could use a cold one," he said feeling his stomach rumble. "And maybe something to eat."

"We got some chili on the stove."

Bubba smiled his assent.

"Cheese and sour cream?"

"Sure."

Focusing on the first sip of his beer, Bubba failed to notice a woman enter the lounge, but when she plunked down beside him, she garnered his complete attention.

"Hope you weren't saving this seat for anyone," she said.

He grinned and shook his head. "I was hopin' someone like you might drop in."

She laughed and offered her hand. "I'm Sheila."

"Will," he said. "But most folks call me Bubba."

"Why's that?"

He shrugged. "It started when I was a kid."

"Do you like it?"

He raised his palms in a gesture of futility.

Sheila gave his arm a gentle squeeze. "Then I think I'll just stick with Will. Besides, you don't look like a Bubba to me."

He felt himself blush though he definitely liked the attention. "Can I buy you a drink?"

"I don't know. The last time I was in here I had a few tequilas too many." She made a face and rubbed her temples. "I should probably stick with something a little lighter."

"Beer?"

"Wine."

He couldn't help but laugh. "City girl, right? I'll bet you grew up with shoes on."

"Most days," she said, her eyes twinkling.

Her dimples left him moonstruck, but when Wanda delivered his chili, he somehow managed to ask her for a wine list.

"You're kiddin', right? A wine *list?*" She looked at Shelia and squinted as if searching her memory. "I thought you were a tequila gal."

"Not anymore."

Wanda gave her an understanding nod. "In that case, I've got two kinds of wine: red and white."

Sheila eyed the bowl of chili. "Which one goes with that?"

"Neither," Wanda said. "But then, you shouldn't ask me. I ain't much of a wine drinker."

"Then make it red, please. And may I have some of what he's having?"

"Sure thing, hon. I'll be right back with both."

Captivated by the woman who had literally just dropped into his life, Bubba strove to make conversation.

Sheila responded in kind, and before long, he had divulged pretty much everything there was to know about the Manager/Caretaker of the Charles County Convention Center

"You actually live there?" she asked.

"For the time being, anyhow. I'm kinda responsible for something the garden club stored there."

"Fascinating," she said. "Tell me about it."

As Bubba provided details, another newcomer arrived. As soon as he spotted the two of them at the bar, he headed their way.

When he reached them, he looked first at Sheila then at Bubba, a frown spreading across his face. Bubba recognized him from his visit to the Convention Center to examine the trophy. He struggled to recall his name. *Marty was it? Or Morty? Something like that.*

Sheila shifted her barstool closer to Bubba, then put her hand on his arm for support. "This might be a wee bit awkward," she whispered, then in a normal voice said, "Will, meet Marty."

"It's *Monty*," the new arrival said as he reached into his pocket. He extracted a pair of panties and dangled them over the bar while looking straight into Sheila's eyes. "You lose somethin'?"

"Not that I recall," she said nonchalantly. She peered at the lingerie for a moment then bobbed her head up and down. "Ah, yes. Now that I think about it, I do remember throwing those away."

Monty suspended them above Bubba's chili. "Well, I sure don't need 'em," he said and let them go.

Bubba snatched the lacy undergarment as it fell and set it aside. He resisted the urge to pound Monty's nose to the back of his skull and opted instead for sarcasm. "They look a bit small for you. And I doubt they're frilly enough."

Sheila giggled.

"I wasn't talkin' to you," Monty said, glaring at him.

"Let it go, Will," Sheila said. "Don't encourage him."

"We got a problem here?" asked Wanda.

Bubba noticed she held an unopened bottle of Jack Daniels by the neck. It made a dandy club.

"You'd best not be botherin' ol' Bubba here," she said, brandishing the bottle. "He's a personal friend of mine."

Monty glowered at her. "Why don't you—"

"And did I mention his uncle's the sheriff? He's another good friend of mine." She raised her cell phone in her other hand. "Fact is, I've got him on speed dial."

"Now listen," Monty began.

"No. *You* listen. Git yourself outta here. You can walk out now, or crawl out later, assuming you're still alive, not that it matters to me. So, what'll it be?"

"You just wait 'til I find out who owns this dump, and I tell 'em how you threatened me."

Wanda grinned. "Trust me. She already knows. And she couldn't care less."

~*~

Willa Mae couldn't quite shake the notion that the city club had something to hide. It only made sense, otherwise they had nothing to lose by opening the contest to everyone. They'd almost certainly end up awarding the prize to a non-member, but that shouldn't have been such a big deal. Surely, they were used to being bested by now; it happened every year.

She reviewed the conversation she'd had with the city club's secretary about the added landscaping bonus awarded to the winner of the contest. She'd never heard of Designs by Donny. It sounded more like something a hairdresser or an interior decorator would display on a storefront. After an extra moment's consideration, she called Don Wolf whose nursery specialized in sprucing up the entryways to various subdivisions.

"Don? This is Willa Mae."

"Who?"

"Willa Mae Sundee. I—"

"Say again?"

"Willa M—"

"Oh, yeah! The redhead. Sorry. Had my mind on something else. What can I do for ya?"

Willa made a conscious effort to avoid sounding irritated. She wasn't the only woman in the county with red hair, even though hers was likely the nicest. "I'm trying to find out about a certain landscaper. I thought you might be able to steer me in the right direction."

"Look no further," Don said. "We can handle any project you've got in mind. Big or small, we handle it all."

"Sounds like a slogan."

"Came up with that all by myself."

"No kidding. Wow. But I'm not looking to hire anyone. I just need to find out who owns an outfit called Designs by Donny."

"I've heard of it," Don said. "The guy's new, small-time. Funny name though."

"Donny?"

"Actually, it's Adonis. Adonis Dorn."

Willa Mae stared straight ahead, seeing nothing. "Did you say *Dorn?*"

"Yeah. D-o-r-n."

"As in *Ramona* Dorn, president of the garden club?"

"Uh-huh. I'm pretty sure she's his momma. Why?"

Willa Mae chuckled. "I was just curious. Thanks, Don. You've been a big help."

The call ended and Willa Mae sat back in her comfy chair trying to decide how best to use the information she'd just gleaned.

Adonis? And a strip show run under the guise of a landscaper? It couldn't get any better.

~*~

"Where are we going?" Ramona asked.

"Atlanta," said Odell. "Well, actually, more like Decatur. Kinda in-between."

They made do with chit-chat while the miles slipped by beneath them. Traffic grew heavier as they approached the city, then seemed to dissipate somewhat as they turned down Ponce De Leon Avenue and pulled into a parking lot at the Yarrab Shrine Temple.

"You're kidding," Ramona said in obvious dismay.

"You're gonna love this," Odell promised. He pulled into an empty space near the back of the lot. Men, women, and children streamed toward a building that could easily have housed a huge mosque.

She looked into his eyes, an expression of disbelief on

her face. "We're going to the circus?"

"Not even close. Just stick with me." He took her hand as they left the car behind and joined the crowd.

They entered a large, well-lighted room with a high ceiling and white walls. Bleachers filled one end of the space and a large, oval shaped track was marked on the floor. Two sets of women wearing outlandish costumes in mostly contrasting colors took up much of the space. All of them wore roller skates and helmets, plus elbow and knee pads. Some had exotic makeup, and many had colorful tattoos. But what really garnered Ramona's attention were the extras they wore, seemingly at random. A few of the skaters sported pastel tutus while others wore fishnet hose or leggings with exotic designs.

"What in the world...." Ramona said as she strained to take it all in and make sense of it.

"Would you like a beer?" Odell asked.

"Uh, sure."

"Wait right here," he said, depositing her in a cushioned seat nearest the edge of the oval. "These are the VIP seats. I wanted you to see this up close."

"VIP? *Up close?*"

He patted her hand and slipped away while she tried to take it all in. In addition to a number on the back of their jerseys, each skater had a name emblazoned above, below or beside the numeral. Ramona felt her eyes grow wide as she read some of the more outrageous ones: Omah Lord, Whutsit2ya, Glama-Zon, and Lady Die.

Though their names all hinted at various shades of monsters, murder, or mayhem, the women all seemed in jovial spirits. Several took laps around the broad oval track, loosening up and chatting as they went. Contestants came in a variety of shapes, sizes, and ethnicities, and most appeared to know each other.

When Odell returned with their beverages, Ramona looked him in the eye. "*Roller Derby?* Seriously? This is your solution to my dilemma?"

He clinked his beer can against hers in an informal toast. "Yep. You're gonna love it; I promise. Just settle back, and I'll try to explain what's going on."

"You've been here often?"

He shook his head. "This is only my second visit, but I suspect I'll be back. And I'm hoping you'll come with me."

"Uh, right," said Ramona, her voice anything but certain.

When the match began, so did Odell. He explained the basics of the sport, which, while maintaining some of the theatrical trappings of pro wrestling and the Hollywood aspects of the competition from its glamour days in the 1960s and early 70s, had evolved into something quite different.

The reborn sport, Odell pointed out, used a flat track rather than a banked one which instantly multiplied the number of potential venues a million-fold. Just as important, the sport was owned and operated by the women who participated in it. They called the shots and made it fun not just to watch, but to compete in, too.

"But it's phony, right?" Ramona said. "Kinda like pro wrestling?"

He shook his head. "No way. These gals are serious. When it comes to the competition, they're all business. Watch; you'll see."

"You're sure they're not rigged?"

Odell grinned. "I'm told they often were in the past. But that's when the skaters were mere employees, actors told to follow a script. Now they're owners. They're in it for the competition and the comradery."

"And the bruises and broken bones?" she asked.

He shrugged. "I admit, it's not a game for the timid or faint-hearted."

She watched as ten skaters arranged themselves at the start of the match. "Okay, so what's up? How does this work?"

"It's pretty simple, really. Each team puts five players on the track, four blockers and a jammer."

Ramona rolled her eyes toward the ceiling. "A *jammer?*"

"They're the ones with a star on their helmets. Their job is to break through the blockers from the other team, then race around the track and pass them. They get a point for each blocker they pass."

"That's it?"

"Pretty much. But breaking through the blockers isn't easy. It's a full contact sport, which is why they wear helmets and pads."

As he spoke a massive collision sent four skaters sprawling, and both jammers raced through the opening. Ramona gripped Odell's arm. "What if someone gets hurt?"

He pointed to the referees and scorers in the center of the oval. "They keep an eye on things and will stop the match if necessary. These women aren't dumb; they've got EMTs standing by, too."

Within a few moments the action stopped.

"What's happening?" Ramona asked. "They were going at it pretty hard."

"It's the end of a jam," said Odell. "A jam only lasts a short time, then fresh skaters come out and the battle continues."

"I find it a little confusing."

"You'll catch on. Just watch. I'm no expert, but I think I've got a handle on it. And even though the penalties seem a little odd, I'm beginning to pick up on them, too."

They continued to watch until halftime when a slender woman wearing the gaudy green and grey colors of the Hotlanta Hip Hops sat down beside Odell. "Sheriff Odum?" she said, extending her hand. "It's good to meet you in person."

Odell introduced her to Ramona as Jocelyn Bishop. "We had a video chat the other day, and she's been kind enough to help me understand the sport."

Ramona shook the woman's hand, somewhat surprised by her gentile grip. "Odell thinks I should host a roller derby event as a fund raiser back home. But I've gotta tell you, this is going to be a hard sell to the members of my garden club. I can't imagine very many of them dressing up, much less wearing skates. And that doesn't begin to cover the idea of a gigantic shoving match on wheels."

Jocelyn's dimples came into full bloom when she smiled, first at Ramona and then at Odell. "I think I can help you with that. In fact, I'm sure of it."

Chapter Seven

"A woman is like a teabag—you can't tell how strong she is until you put her in hot water." – Eleanor Roosevelt

Sheila found it much less taxing to spend an evening without having an ulterior motive. She couldn't recall the last time she'd had the luxury. Nor did it hurt that her new friend, Will "Bubba" Broome, the county convention center's Chief Cook and Bottle Washer, just happened to be kinda cute. And lonely.

She especially liked that he didn't try to pass himself off as someone else, someone important or well-to-do. He treated her well, demonstrated a rare degree of courtesy, and just happened to be comfortably well-connected to a bar owner *and* the head of local law enforcement. Clearly, Will/Bubba was a worthy companion.

Going back to "his place," which he quickly pointed out belonged to the good citizens of Charles County, turned out to be a no-brainer, and one which required precisely no pre-planning or play-acting.

Though he offered to drive her to the Center, Sheila knew better. She simply followed him in her own car in case she discovered she'd misjudged him, and considering her recent encounter with Monty, or whatever his name was, she'd lost confidence in her ability to rate the safety of potential dates. Besides, unlike the evening she spent with the pantie dropper—the mere thought of which made her wince—she fully intended to survey the landscape before she committed to any sort of romance.

Will warned her the Center might be in need of some clean-up since the Jaycees weren't always in the best condition for managing such chores when they wrapped up an evening that featured alcohol and grilled meat. The couple stood outside the venue trying to assess the amount of exterior work needed.

"I wouldn't mind helping you straighten up a little," she told him.

He focused puppy dog eyes on her. "Nah. I couldn't let you do that. Wouldn't be right."

"You're sweet, but I won't let you do it all alone. Besides, I have a confession to make," she said, feeling a rare twinge of guilt. "I already knew about the trophy. In fact, I'm a member of the club. I joined just a short time ago."

He shrugged it off as if used to such minor breaches of honesty. "As long as we're being up front," he said, "I should probably admit I'm totally into beautiful brunettes."

They entered the Charles County Convention Center arm-in-arm.

~*~

The following afternoon, a smiling Ramona welcomed the members of the garden club's executive committee into her living room for a third emergency meeting. She had to use her dining room chairs to accommodate everyone, but she had no intention of inviting spectators. Her smile

97

dissolved, however, when she saw Constance DuBois enter the room while deep in conversation with Marlie, the club's secretary.

Once everyone settled in, Ramona called attention to her guest, Jocelyn Bishop. "I'm pleased to introduce you to my new friend, Anti-Maim." She held up an 8-by-10, glossy, color photo of the skater with her name emblazoned across the top. Both Ramona and Jocelyn beamed while everyone else in the room tried to stifle smirks.

"Her real name is Jocelyn Bishop, but when she's competing, Anti-Maim is the name on her jersey, right next to a great big number 1."

"I don't understand," said Marlie. "Are you a soccer player?"

Jocelyn chuckled. "Nope. I'm a skater, a blocker actually, for the Hotlanta Hip Hops."

Most everyone in the room shared confused looks and whispered consultations. Ramona let it go on for a minute or so, then called everyone back to order.

"Jocelyn is in charge of outreach for her Roller Derby team. She has a proposal for a fund raiser that I believe can resolve all the hubbub that's arisen because of the contest Hildie left us with," Ramona said.

"If you think I'm gonna get up on roller skates, you're crazy!" opined Constance. "I could break my neck."

Ramona thought that option had a definite appeal, but she was quick to allay the fear spreading through the committee that they'd all be recruited for the match.

"Relax, Connie. We need two club members to participate in the actual match. They'll have to be able to skate, of course, and be healthy enough to compete. I imagine that lets out most of our membership." Ramona turned to Jocelyn. "I think I've scared 'em enough. Why don't you continue?"

"Gladly. We're trying to get the word out about our sport; it's so much better than it used to be, and you'd be amazed to learn how fast it's spreading. It's growing mostly in urban areas, but our goal is to spread it even farther. We want to hold exhibition matches and build interest all over, but we need help to let folks know about us. That's why we're willing to compete for charity. We benefit from bringing the sport to new fans, and you benefit by sponsoring a unique charity event that no one around here has ever done before."

"So, we don't actually have to skate?" Marlie asked.

"We'd like to have a few local skaters in the match," Jocelyn said. "That makes it much more interesting. Local people like to see local skaters, but they also want to see some big-league athletes."

Constance spoke up. "Will the county club sponsor a team, too?"

"I hope so," Ramona said. "But I haven't spoken to them yet."

"We want the match to be genuine and entertaining, so that means we need good skaters," Jocelyn said. "My team is willing to make the trip, and I spoke with my counterpart who skates for a team in Savannah. They're willing to meet us for a showdown right here in St. Charlotte."

"How's this going to solve our gardening contest problem?" Constance asked. "It sounds to me like all we're doing is promoting this ridiculous Roller Derby thing."

"It's not ridiculous," Ramona said. "And don't forget, we're doing it for a great cause."

"Okay, so we also raise some money for a playground. That still doesn't resolve whether or not the gardening contest will be private or open to the world." Constance was on her feet, her fists planted firmly on her hips.

Ramona didn't back down. "If each club comes up with two skaters, we can make it work. The thing is, all four would have to compete as jammers."

Constance appeared to be winding up again, so Ramona hurried on. "On the track, each team has a jammer and four blockers, a total of ten skaters at a time. The jammers try to work their way past the other team's blockers, skate around the track, and do it again. They score one point for every blocker they pass."

Jocelyn chimed in. "We'll tally the points made by each club's jammer."

Ramona continued, "Whichever club's jammers score the most points, wins. Their club gets to decide if the gardening contest is open or closed."

"I don't like it," Constance said.

"Too bad you're not on the Executive Committee," Marlie said. "You don't get a vote."

Ramona tried to keep from smiling while Constance scowled. "It's not just me; this should go before the entire club for a vote."

"That's not why we were elected." Ramona responded. "Besides, we're running out of time, and this seems to me to be an excellent way to proceed."

Ramona asked for a volunteer to put the proposal in the form of a motion, which they did. It was quickly seconded Constance demanded an opportunity to discuss it further, but the climate in the room had clearly turned against her. If she had any supporters, Ramona couldn't spot them. The motion passed in a landslide.

Ramona thanked the committee, then added, "Now all we need is for the county club to agree to it, but really, what choice do they have? If they want a shot at the contest, they'll have to take their lumps on the track."

Jocelyn gave Ramona an approving look. "Girl, I *like* the way you think! Now tell me, do you know how to skate?"

~*~

Sheila couldn't sleep despite being in a comfortable bed with Will who slept soundly. It was their second night together. They stayed in that evening because no events were scheduled at the convention center, and Will insisted he had to stick around to keep an eye on the garden club's trophy.

They'd found enough to drink, thanks to the leftovers provided by the Jaycees, and they'd both enjoyed an amorous romp that should have left her smiling as she slept.

Instead, she lay awake wondering what on Earth had happened to her. She'd clearly lost her edge. Instead of plotting a means to enrich herself, she'd been thinking about where she and Will might grab breakfast, assuming she could talk him into leaving the Center for a while.

She hadn't packed anything but sweats and other comfy stuff, and she definitely needed a change of clothes. She wondered what sort of outfit might help keep him interested in her. From the way he talked, she didn't think he was he seeing anyone else, but could she be sure of that? And what did he really think about her? Had she moved too fast? Would he think she was too easy? She'd practically moved in with him!

Will rolled over, put his hand on her hip, and gave her

a gentle squeeze. "You're amazing," he said.

"So are you," she murmured, but he gave no indication he'd heard her. As far as she could tell, he'd gone way beyond the sheep counting stage and was well into dreamland.

Sheila stared up at the dark ceiling and commanded herself to chill out. It didn't work. A tiny light in the corner of the room, probably attached to a smoke detector, seemed excessively bright. And the sound of an occasional car passing by seemed unreasonably loud. As did the ticking of a clock somewhere else. Where had that been? And what would she do for a toothbrush? Would he want to kiss her when he first woke up? How icky would that be?

And yet, how romantic?

The last time she woke up in a lover's bed, the only thing she sought was escape. Now she was worried about choosing between scrambled eggs *a la* Convention Center and a decent breakfast at a diner in town.

What the heck is the matter with me?

She left the question unanswered because a new sound grabbed her attention. The noise associated with breaking glass was anything but a novelty to her. She'd broken windows before and knew the sound well. Best done with an elbow, preferably one covered with a jacket or sweatshirt, the blow required little effort. The sound of breaking glass was typically followed by the sound of a hand fumbling with a deadbolt or scrabbling about in search of a doorknob.

Sheila heard both.

"Will!" she whispered as she grabbed his shoulder and gave him a shake. "Someone's trying to break in!"

~*~

"What're you grinning about?" Ramona asked. She reached across the bedsheet and gave Odell a nudge.

He eased up on one elbow and looked into her eyes. "I haven't seen you this animated since I wined and dined you in the park. I don't suppose it has anything to do with me, does it?"

"Hardly." She frowned theatrically. "And since when does fruit and cheese amount to 'dining?'"

"Hey, there was wine, too! Don't forget that."

"You're right; there was," she said. "And, I'm willing to admit, it wasn't awful."

He shook his head. "You're a hard woman to please, Miz Dorn."

"We'll be fine as long as you keep tryin'."

He flopped back onto his pillow. "I'm exhausted from the effort."

"Liar." She poked him and giggled.

Unwilling to admit he actually was tired, Odell changed the topic. "So, the ladies in your club are okay with the Roller Derby idea?"

"Oh, yeah. I had my doubts at first, but as they heard the details, I could tell most of the committee members were clearly intrigued, especially when they heard they wouldn't have to join in the mayhem. Jocelyn shared video of a recent match and a few interviews with some of the skaters. I thought the younger members would be the ones to get excited about it, but really, everyone thought it looked like fun. Except Constance. I don't think she understands the concept of fun."

He chuckled. "Hopefully, now it'll be easier going forward."

"Speaking of which," Ramona said in a low voice as she rolled toward him, extended her arm, and slowly stroked his thigh. "I have an itty-bitty request, a little something I thought we could try."

"Oh. Well... Uh—" Before he could respond, his cell phone rang.

"*Oh, come on,*" Ramona groused. "It's nearly two AM, and I'm wide awake!"

"Sorry, babe," he said. "I guess bad guys can't tell time. I've gotta take this."

He picked up the phone, noted the caller ID and said, "Sheriff Odum. This had better be good, son."

"It's me, Bubba."

"Yeah, I know." Odell squinted at the clock; Ramona was right. "Can't you tell time? What's the big—"

"We had a break-in."

"Oh, geez. Are you okay?"

"Yeah. We're fine, but the guy who broke in isn't. Sheila got him with my shotgun."

"Dear lord! You *shot* someone?"

"Me? No. That was Sheila. But it's not—"

"Did you call for an ambulance?"

"Of course."

"And who the hell is Sheila?"

Bubba sighed. "I'll explain it all when you get here. Just hurry, okay?"

Odell didn't respond. Instead, he dressed as quickly as possible, made his apologies to Ramona, and hurried toward the door.

"At least give me a kiss goodbye," she said, having wrapped herself in a bathrobe while he strapped on his badge and gun.

"Believe me," he said after a too-short kiss. "I'd much rather stay here with you."

"Can't you send someone? You're the boss, right? The top dog?"

"Well, yeah, but this involves family, to say nothing of a gunshot victim. I can't leave this for a deputy."

He hurried out her front door as Ramona's son, Donny, called out, "Is everything okay?"

"Call me when you can," Ramona yelled.

Odell waved, climbed in his patrol car, flipped on the blue lights, and took off down the street. He would have used his siren, too, but doing so this late at night in a residential neighborhood would only have generated complaints. He waited until he was out on the highway leading to the convention center before kicking in the siren.

When he arrived, a pair of EMTs strolled out of the building chatting amiably. He stopped them with a raised palm. "Where's the vic?"

"Good question. Ask the couple inside."

Since there were no other first responder vehicles in sight, Odell assumed the EMT referred to his nephew. He hurried through the still open door to the foyer and called out, "Bubba? Where are you?"

"In here, Uncle Odell," came the reply. "We're in the main hall."

Odell hustled through the double doors and immediately spotted Bubba and a woman standing near the garden club's trophy. There didn't seem to be an emergency, so he slowed to a walk. "What's going on?" he asked. "I thought you said someone got shot."

"I'm sorry," Bubba said. "In all the confusion, that sorta came out wrong. I didn't mean Sheila *shot* him. She used my gun to hit him in the head."

"It was dark," the woman said. She looked disheveled and visibly upset. "I'm Sheila."

"I kinda figured that." He pursed his lips and looked at Bubba. "So, where's the guy she whacked?"

"He's— Uh, actually, I dunno. Gone."

Odell tilted his head as he gazed at his nephew to see if his pupils were dilated. They appeared normal. "How 'bout you run that by me one more time. Maybe with some detail."

The woman piped up. "Like I said, it was dark. I heard some noise, like glass breaking, so I tried to wake Will up, but he was really sound asleep."

"I may have had a little too much to drink." Bubba looked distinctly sheepish.

Odell ignored him and focused on her. "And? When you couldn't wake this knucklehead up? Then what?"

"*I* got up. To, you know, investigate."

"Dressed like that?" Odell tried not to stare at her. She wore one of Bubba's thin T-shirts, and the covering provided precious little in the way of modesty.

"I wasn't dressing for a party; I grabbed the first thing I could find," she said. "And when I went to the door, I stubbed my toe on something. I didn't know what it was at first—"

"Because of the dark?"

"Right. But when I reached down and felt it, I knew right away it was some kind of rifle."

"Shotgun," interjected Bubba. "My Remington 20-gauge."

"Whatever," She said. "Anyway, I picked it up and took it with me even though I had no idea how to use it. I couldn't tell if there were bullets in it or anything."

Bubba put his arm around her. "Shells, darlin', not bullets. Remind me to take you shooting sometime."

She gave him a confused look, then went on. "I figured if someone really had broken in, they wouldn't know if I knew how to use the gun or not."

"And you intended to get the drop on 'em, right?" Odell asked.

"Well, yeah. I guess."

"Just like in the Old West."

Bubba frowned at that. "Hey now, there's no need to get snarky."

"And what if the intruder also had a gun?" Odell asked. "One which he most likely knew how to use?"

She nodded. "Actually, that very thought went through my mind. So, when I finally did see there was someone in the building, I didn't say anything. I snuck up behind him as quiet as I could and—"

"This is the part that makes me so proud," Bubba said, giving her a squeeze. "Go on, hon'."

"Well, I sorta hit him in the head."

"With the shotgun." Odell meant it as a statement

rather than a question.

"Yeah. I used it like a baseball bat. Hit him with the wooden part."

"The stock," added Bubba.

"I was shaking so bad I was afraid I might miss him, but I didn't. He went down like I'd killed him. Limp as linguine. That's when I screamed."

Odell glanced at Bubba. "And that was enough to wake you up?"

"Probably. I dunno. She came back into my room, dropped the shotgun, and started shakin' me like crazy. She was crying and carryin' on something awful. I could see she was scared out of her mind. Kept sayin' she'd killed somebody."

"And that's when you called 911?"

"Yeah. I grabbed the shotgun, and we stayed in the room in case he got up and came after us."

"You didn't go in and check on him?"

"Hell no! He broke in on us, remember?"

"I get it," Odell said. "And when did you think to call me?"

"After the cops left."

Odell made a mental note to check the duty roster to see who answered the call. "And the EMTs? They just hung around?"

"They talked to us for a while after they helped the cops look for the guy Sheila hit. We couldn't see into the hall very well from my room, so we don't know if he got up and walked out, or crawled, or what. He didn't make much noise."

"He didn't make *any* noise," Sheila said. "That's why we thought he was still out there."

"So, he just disappeared into thin air?"

Sheila narrowed her eyes as she looked at him. "I didn't make this up."

"I didn't say—"

"There's some blood on the floor near the stupid trophy," she said. "And some more on the shotgun." She leaned into Bubba. "And neither of us is bleeding."

Odell exhaled. "You must've hit him pretty hard."

"Darn right," she said, defiantly. "As hard as I could."

~*~

Willa Mae didn't recognize the number on her cell phone when it rang but answered it anyway. With any luck, it would be Publisher's Clearing House calling to say she'd won a bazillion dollars a year for life.

"Hullo?"

"I'm trying to reach Mrs. Sundee. This is Ramona Dorn with the—"

"Saint Charlotte Garden Club. I know. I wondered when you'd bother to call."

"I'm sorry. Did I catch you at a bad time?"

"No," said Willa Mae. "Go on."

"I can call back later if it would be more convenient."

"Will you please just get on with it?" *Geez.*

"I'm calling about the contest our late club president sponsored, the Hildegard Henderson Horticultural Award."

"Unless you're calling to tell me it's open to the public,

I'm not interested." *There. Take that!*

"Actually, that *is* the reason I called."

"I'd like a copy of the rules," Willa Mae said. "Only this time, you can bring them to me. I'm not gonna waste another trip into town like last time."

There was a brief pause before Ramona answered. "I'm sorry about that. I had no intention of standing you up. I apologize. Something came up at the last minute."

An empty wine bottle, as I recall, thought the county gardener. "Whatever. Apology accepted. Now, about the rules—"

"We've decided to make this whole affair a bit more interesting," Ramona said. "I don't know if you saw it or not, but there was an editorial in the paper recently that didn't paint a very flattering picture of our club."

"Really?" Willa Mae tried to sound surprised. "I must've missed it. Living so far out here in the wilderness, we hardly ever see the printed word."

Another silence followed before Ramona continued. "Anyway, we think we've found a way to make this work to everyone's advantage."

Willa Mae sat quietly while Ramona went on to explain about the need for a playground for special needs kids and the plan to raise money by staging a Roller Derby event.

"That all sounds real nice," Willa Mae said, "and I'm sure there are a bunch of deserving children who would benefit, but what does it have to do with the gardening contest?"

"This is where it gets interesting," Ramona said. "Each of our clubs will need to find a couple skaters, and their efforts will determine who gets to decide if the contest is open to the public or not." She went on to explain the process in more detail.

For most of her adult life, Willa Mae had avoided being shocked into utter silence. This time, she failed.

"Are you still there?" Ramona asked when she'd gone over everything.

"Yeah."

"Well, what do you think?"

"You really wanna know?"

"Of course."

"I think you're absolutely, totally, and undeniably insane."

~*~

The group Hildie joined for the Holy Land trip came from a small Baptist church on the outskirts of town. Two of the other travelers knew her from the garden club, but none of them were close friends.

The church bus carried them to the International terminal at the Atlanta airport where they disembarked and cued up in front of a guide from the travel agency who would accompany them and handle all their travel needs. He took care of their luggage, answered questions, calmed nerves, and generally provided the homey security the mostly aging travelers needed.

Hildie pulled the young man aside for a brief consultation. "I know you're terribly busy, but I have a problem and need your help." Before he could object, she tucked a wad of hundred-dollar bills in his hand.

"The thing is," she said, "I'm not feeling well, but it's imperative that I take this trip, whether I catch the flight we're booked on or another one."

The man looked confused. "Surely, you—"

"I'm going to do my level best to go with the rest of the group but—" she clutched her stomach. "I have issues."

"If you miss this flight, it will cost a fortune to get on the next one," he said.

She pushed a few more Franklins into his hand. "That won't be a problem. Just see that my luggage is put on the ship, and if possible, check me in."

"That'll require a passport," he said, "and identification."

"It's all in my suitcase," she assured him. "And I have photocopies in my purse. Can I count on you to take care of this for me?"

"I—"

"Please?"

He glanced down at the money in his hand, then looked up at her and nodded.

The faithful passed through security and marched to the gate where they waited patiently to board their aircraft. Hildie waited with them at the back of the line. When the gate agent had checked her in and waved her toward the passage to the plane, Hildie stopped, clutched her stomach, and pretended she was about to throw up.

Begging forgiveness, she left the bewildered gate agent and took a staggered step toward the nearest restroom. A member of her group offered to go with her, but the gate agent wouldn't allow it. The tour guide waved at her and smiled. "I've got you covered," he said.

Hildie promised to return as soon as possible while the agent went back to work processing other passengers. Meanwhile, Hildie dialed a ride share service and hurried toward the exit.

Chapter Eight

"The age of a woman doesn't mean a thing. The best tunes are played on the oldest fiddles." – Ralph Waldo Emerson

Bubba waved to Odell when he entered the Convention Center later the same day. "I'm sorry about you havin' to come out here so early," Bubba said. "I just— I dunno. I wasn't sure what else to do."

"Don't worry about it. You did the right thing." Odell looked around the spacious room. "Where's Shirley?"

"It's Sheila."

"Right, right. I knew that."

"She's out. Said she needed to grab some clothes and do some shopping. I told her we had food, but were runnin' low on beer and toilet paper."

"Sounds very domestic."

Bubba grinned. "Yeah, it does, doesn't it?" He shoved his hands in the pockets of his jeans and wandered toward the trophy at the front of the room which he and Sheila had covered with a table cloth. "This thing is turning out to be a major pain in the butt."

"Break-ins happen," Odell said.

"Not here, they don't. Leastwise, not until that darned thing showed up." He swatted at the drape covering the gaudy prize. "I had an idea, though."

"Oh, Lord," Odell muttered, shaking his head. "But don't keep me in suspense. Let's hear it."

"What if we stored the trophy in your office until the contest is over? Nobody'd be crazy enough to break in there."

Odell scratched his jaw. His five o'clock shadow had darkened since the wee hours. "You know that ain't gonna happen."

"Aw c'mon. Surely, you've got a closet or a storage room or something I could use. The county doesn't pay me to do guard duty. The National Guard does though, and that's one weekend every month. Who's gonna look after it then? And besides, I've got someone else in my life now. I need some free time."

Odell didn't look terribly sympathetic. "You know, of course, that this isn't my problem."

"Yeah, I know," he said, trying not to sound overly dejected.

Odell lightly tapped Bubba's chest. "You need to talk to the garden club. It's their problem. They shouldn't have dropped this in your lap. You're not getting anything out of it."

Bubba's mood lightened instantly. "You're right. I just need to call them and tell 'em to haul this thing outta here."

"On the other hand," Odell said, "you might want to consider charging them for providing security."

Bubba gave the idea some consideration before

rejecting it. "If I did that, I'd still be stuck here." He felt the room closing in on him again. "I don't want that. I need to be able to spend some time with—"

"Sher— Sheila."

"Bingo."

"Has she moved in?"

"Sorta. She's got a tiny place she rents by the week. Says she can't stand it there." Bubba waved toward what the county called the Grand Ballroom. "We got more space than we need here."

"All this is kinda sudden, isn't it? I mean, you hardly know the girl."

"I know enough. And after the way she handled herself last night... Well, a girl like that doesn't drop into your life every day. I'm gonna hang onto her."

Odell nodded. "That's understandable. She'd be quite a catch under any circumstances. It's just that—"

"What?"

"Think about it. She shows up on Monday, and twenty-four hours later someone tries to steal the garden club trophy, only she's on hand to save the day. It feels a little too convenient to me, that's all. I'm not a big believer in coincidence."

"You think she had something to do with the break-in?"

Odell shook his head emphatically. "I'm not sayin' that."

"Then, what *are* you sayin'?"

"Oh, I don't know. It probably doesn't mean a thing. Just me bein' suspicious. It's a cop thing."

"Well, maybe you need to find a girlfriend of your own.

Maybe then you wouldn't be so ready to jump to conclusions."

Odell appeared to be trying, but failing, to suppress a grin. "Y'know, you could be right."

Having convinced herself that Ramona Dorn and the rest of the Saint Charlatans were certifiably nuts, Willa Mae felt a sense of relief. If they didn't want to open their stupid contest to the world, then so be it. She wasn't about to help them put a happy face on it by hosting something as ridiculous as the Roller Derby.

As if by magic, Jim Croce's "Roller Derby Queen" began playing on her car radio. Though she often listened to a golden oldies station, Willa Mae hadn't heard that particular tune in years. She found herself tapping her fingers on the steering wheel as she made her way to Wolf's Nursery for birdseed and plant food.

Roller Derby? Was the tune some kind of sign?

The mere thought struck her as absurd. Besides, who in the world did Ramona and her minions expect to compete? Though she had no way of actually calculating it, Willa Mae assumed the average age of her membership was fifty-something or higher. Though she imagined herself one of the younger members, she still couldn't see herself on skates. The very idea made her....

What?

She had done a good bit of skating when growing up. Like bike riding, it wasn't something one was likely to forget, even if it had been a while since her last outing.

And just exactly how long ago had that been? She searched her memory and quickly found the answer. It had been roughly a year since her daughter asked to celebrate her birthday with a party at a skating rink on the edge of town. It was the only skating rink in the county, as far as Willa Mae knew. And, most likely, the closest one for skaters in all the surrounding counties.

So, how, she wondered, did they stay in business? Obviously, people liked to skate, preferably without getting run over by cars or trucks. Whoever owned the place probably made a killing on equipment rental and concessions. Was that where Derby Dorn and her maniacal minions planned to stage their event? If so, the location would automatically make it a townie event; county folk weren't needed, or wanted. If Willa Mae promoted a skating event she'd use the National Guard Armory which sat smack in the middle of the county, and anyone who found the place would be welcome.

She let the whole thing go as she pulled into the parking lot at her destination. Wolf's Nursery had the distinction of being the only place in the county which carried the birdseed brand she preferred, and even though the store catered mostly to residents of St. Charlotte, Willa Mae still shopped there. She knew exactly where to find everything she needed.

With an extra-large bag of birdseed and fifty pounds of fertilizer in her cart, Willa Mae approached the cash register. The store's owner, Don Wolf, was listening to the comments of a heavyset woman she didn't recognize. The woman made no effort to keep her voice down as she pointed to one of the signs Willa Mae had distributed.

"I can't believe the gall of these rednecks," the woman said. "Why can't they sponsor their own contest? Why do they have to push their way into ours? The whole thing infuriates me."

"Is it really that big a deal?" the store owner asked.

"Big? No. It's huge! You should see the trophy."

"I've heard about it, Mrs. DuBois, but I haven't actually seen—"

"Take it from me. It's enormous. And tacky, of course." She stared up at the ceiling and back down again. "But it's a prestige thing, a chance to have one's garden designated as special, above the rest." She took a breath. "I've seen the competition, and just between you and me, there isn't much."

Willa Mae couldn't stand to remain silent. "Is that why you don't want the contest open to everyone? Because it'd be too much competition?"

The woman turned her head slowly, stopping when she had Willa Mae square in her sights. "Are you talking to me?"

"Do you see anyone else in line?"

She sniffed in response, then gazed down into Willa Mae's cart. "You realize birdseed attracts rats, don't you? I understand that's an enormous problem out in the country."

Willa Mae ground her teeth.

The woman went on. "Your kind only care about vegetables. This contest is about landscape, flowers, shrubs, beauty. I can't imagine why you'd be in the least bit interested."

"Will that be all, Miz DuBois?" the merchant asked.

"Indeed," she said, handing him a credit card.

When the transaction was complete, she waltzed through the front entrance without a backward glance.

"What a pompous ass," Willa Mae said, then corrected

herself. "On second thought, make that a cow. Donkeys have more sense."

Wolf appeared not to have heard her. "We need all the customers we can get," he said as he rang up her purchases. "Can I give you a hand loading that stuff in your car?"

"I'm stronger than I look," she said, beginning to reconsider her rejection of the Roller Derby idea. "Way stronger."

~*~

Ramona slept late, something she'd planned on, though she hadn't intended to do it alone. She hadn't known Odell very long, but their mutual attraction felt as real as anything she'd ever experienced. That included her former husband. If not for Donny, she'd have precious little to show for the years she wasted with his father.

By contrast, Odell was kind, considerate, and not at all bad looking, to say nothing of his skills in the bedroom. Whatever he lacked in experience he made up for in zeal, and he put his own satisfaction second to hers. Plus, he not only knew how to cook, he was willing to help with the dishes. As astonishing a man as she could imagine, she had no idea how he had remained single. And for that, she felt amply grateful.

Her cell phone interrupted her thoughts, and she answered it with a sigh followed by, "Hello?"

"Ramona? This is Willa Mae."

Closing her eyes, Ramona shifted into a different mental gear. "Yes, of course. Willa Mae. We spoke yester—"

"I've changed my mind," the caller said. "About this Roller Derby thing."

"Oh? That's great. Let's—"

"I've got some conditions, however."

"We really do need to go over all the details," Ramona said, hurrying to squeeze her words in.

"First off, it's gotta be held at the National Guard Armory."

Though she'd driven by the place on occasion, Ramona had never been inside. "Is that something they'd even allow?"

"Sure," said Willa Mae. "My husband knows the guy in charge, Major Something-or-other. He'll go along."

"Okay, but—"

"Item number two," Willa Mae said. "If you expect my club to get behind this charity deal, then it shouldn't matter who scores the most runs, or points, or whatever it is they count in Roller Derby. If we participate in the skating, then we get to participate in the garden contest, too. It's all or nothing."

Ramona felt trapped, and while she realized the proposal was essentially quite fair, she also knew she'd brought the whole thing on herself. Now she'd have to pay the piper. "I'll need to run it by the Executive Committee before I can give you a firm answer," she said.

"I understand. I'd have to do the same thing here. Now, there's just one other detail. I won't ask anyone else from my club to skate. I won't have them risking life and limb just to make me happy. I expect you may feel the same way. So, when it comes to skaters from the clubs, it's gotta be just you and me."

It took a moment for Ramona to realize her jaw had dropped open.

"Excuse me?"

"You heard what I said. Just you and me. We'll be the... What'd you call 'em?"

"Jammers?"

"Yeah."

"But I'm not—"

"Can you skate?" asked Willa Mae.

"Yes, but—"

"How old are you?"

Ramona glared at the phone. "What's *that* go to do with anything?"

"I'm forty-five," Willa Mae said. "I've got two kids, and I'm in okay shape, though it's been a long time since I got up on skates. I heard you have a son who's old enough to run his own business, but I wanna make sure you and I are about the same age."

Ramona muttered, "We are."

"Well then, unless you're disabled, you oughta be willing to accept the challenge."

"I, uhm... I'd like a little time to think it over," Ramona said, wondering how in the world she might get out of it. "How 'bout I call you back tomorrow? It's not just me; I need to check with our Derby contact to make sure having only two local skaters would be okay. She said we needed two from each club."

Willa Mae snorted into the phone. "Do whatever you've gotta do. Then call me back. I'll be waiting."

<Click>

Ramona felt as if she'd been run over by a truck. Or a runaway freight train. She and Jocelyn had joked about

Ramona competing in a match, but the reality of actually doing it never entered her mind. Now it had.

And it terrified her.

~*~

Odell checked the duty roster and reviewed the call report turned in by the two deputies who responded to the break-in at the Convention Center. Though satisfied with their write-up, he was annoyed that they'd been unable to figure out who did it.

If he ran a big city operation, it would be possible to get DNA from one of the bloodstains and run it against the various criminal databases available. In a town like St. Charlotte, that option was reserved for major crimes like murder or kidnaping. As a result, the blood sample they'd collected sat in an evidence bag on a shelf in the evidence locker, a room at the rear of his office. Useless.

He noted a line near the end of the report which stated that their efforts to obtain fingerprints had turned up too many to be of use. Since just about every civic and service club in the county held their meetings there, that made perfect, if utterly maddening sense.

Simply being annoyed didn't accomplish anything, and Odell had long ago learned how to channel his disappointment into a closed compartment. He'd had plenty of practice.

"Odell! You busy?" asked Minnie Harlow, who ran the office and maintained what passed for decorum in the department. She leaned back in her chair just far enough to see through Odell's open door. "There's a woman here to see ya. Says her name's Dorn."

Odell got up and hurried to the front of the building

where Ramona sat on a bench near the wall. She had an odd look on her face, so he tried to lighten the moment. "Hey there! Fancy meeting you here. I don't see any handcuffs, so it must not be too serious. What're you in for?"

Startled, she seemed to grope for something to say.

"It was a joke," he said. "Not a very good one, I admit."

She rewarded him with a weak smile. When she stood up, he gave her a hug which she returned with surprising force. That triggered an alarm in his head.

"Are you okay?"

She shrugged. "I dunno. Maybe, I guess."

He put his arm around her shoulders and guided her toward his office. As they passed Minnie's desk, Odell told her to hold his calls. Minnie dipped an eyebrow as if evaluating his companion, then gave him an affirmative nod.

"Have a seat." He gestured to the only other chair in his office then settled into his own behind the desk. "Now then, what's up? Why so glum?"

"It's the Derby. I'm going to have to skate in it, and to be honest, that scares the bejeezus outta me."

He figured any smile he mustered would likely be misconstrued and so maintained a neutral expression. "No one can make you do anything you don't want to do."

"I know," she said. "But I still feel trapped." She explained Willa Mae's demand that only the two of them battle it out, winner take all. "If I don't skate, we'll have to call the whole thing off."

Odell pondered the problem. "Could you get someone to take your place? This Willa person hasn't ever met you, has she?"

"No, but something like that wouldn't stay a secret for very long." She frowned at him. "Besides, don't you think that's unethical?"

"Well, yeah. I suppose."

"And you're a cop. Shame on you."

She said it with a little smile, so he didn't take her seriously. "You're right. That'd be cheesy. Forget I suggested it."

"Done."

"Are you afraid you'll get hurt?"

"Yes! Some of the women I saw in the video are way bigger than me, and they've been skating for quite a while. I haven't been on skates in years."

"We can start fixing that tonight, if you'd like," he said. "I haven't skated in a long time either. We could pop over to that roller rink by the high school."

"Tonight?"

"Sure. Why not?"

"Willa said I had to skate against her unless I had a disability," Ramona said. "I don't suppose just being chicken would count."

"Probably not," he said. "So, let's do this: After work, I'll swing by my place and change then pick you up around 6. We can grab a bite to eat before or after we skate, whichever you'd like. How's that sound?"

"It sounds like you have more faith in me than I do."

He gave her a huge smile. "Hey. Trust me on this. I know a winner when I see one."

~*~

Sheila put the finishing touches on the two bacon lettuce, and tomato sandwiches she'd made while Will distributed plates, napkins, and utensils. Lacking a table in Will's makeshift office/apartment, they took their meals on a table in the Center's central hall.

"I figured out how to get rid of that stupid trophy," he said while wiping mayo from his lip. "I'm going to ask the garden club to come and get it out of here. That'll leave us free to go someplace fun whenever we want."

Sheila tried not to look surprised or disappointed; she hadn't completely given up on the idea of stripping the trophy of its jewels. "Do you think that's a good idea?"

"Well, yeah. Don't you? I wouldn't have to spend all my time guarding it."

She shrugged. "That'd be nice. On the other hand...."

"What?"

It hurt her soul to see someone so eager to be used. "Have you ever really looked at that trophy?"

"Sure, I see it every day."

"I'm talking about a really deep look, an examination."

Will set his sandwich down and poked an escaping slice of tomato back into position. "It's loaded with jewels and stuff. It's gotta be worth a lot, which is why that guy tried to steal it."

"But you don't really know how much it's worth. No one's mentioned a dollar figure, have they?"

"Not to me," he said.

Sheila tapped her front teeth with a manicured fingernail as she considered how best to continue. "I'm no expert, but I can tell you the gems on that trophy would easily

126

sell for a few grand." Enough, she thought, for a really delightful week at the beach, or maybe a more reliable car to replace the shaky pile of automotive parts she'd been driving.

"What're you drivin' at?" Will asked as he prepared to take another bite of his sandwich. "My uncle suggested I keep it here and charge the garden club for guarding it."

"That's a great idea!"

He looked at her as if he'd been betrayed. "No, it's not!"

"Hear me out, okay?" She took a deep breath and hoped Will would be easy to sway. "By keeping the trophy here, we'd have all the time in the world to carefully remove those gemstones and replace them with the kind of stuff used in costume jewelry. Not only would we have the cash from the sale of the stones, but we'd get paid for the time needed to… *liberate* them."

Will stopped chewing and stared at her. "Liberate?"

"Okay. Steal."

"Holy crap," he said, his mouth and eyes still open. He seemed to be searching the cavernous room for eavesdroppers or listening devices.

"Y'know what?" Sheila said, her words rushed. "Never mind. It was a stupid idea. I'm embarrassed I even brought it up. You probably think—"

Will recovered and chuckled. "Back when I first saw that thing, I had some thoughts of my own about grabbin' it and takin' off." He waved his hand in a sweeping gesture that took in the whole room. "This place isn't my idea of paradise, but until I met you, I was content to make do."

"And now?"

"Well, things are different now."

"How so?" she asked.

"I can't just look out for myself anymore."

Sheila stepped around the corner of the table, wrapped her arms around him, and planted a world class kiss on his lips.

~*~

Willa Mae gave a small but triumphant snort when she saw Ramona Dorn's name and number on the screen of her cell phone. The call came in right on time. "Are we good to go?" she asked without preamble.

"Yes. I spoke with Jocelyn Bishop, our contact with the Hotlanta Hip Hops."

"Sounds more like a rap music band," Willa Mae commented.

"I guess. Anyway, she said we could make it work. I told her you wanted to stage the match at the National Guard Armory, and she said that was okay, too, provided we could get permission. I'm going to leave that part up to you. I also did a phone poll of the Executive Committee, and they're all okay with the arrangement."

Ramona paused for a moment. "One of the members suggested something else, though. It's a condition you'll have to agree to."

"What's that?"

"The garden contest goes on first, the trophy will be awarded at the end of the Derby event. Like you said, all or nothing."

"I'm sure my club will go along with that," Willa Mae said. "But I've got to say, you've really surprised me. I thought for sure you'd back out."

"Why's that?"

"I don't know. Just a feeling."

"Well," Ramona said, "when the time comes, and we're racing around that track, I imagine you'll get plenty more feelings, so be prepared."

"What d'ya mean by that?"

"It's a rough and tumble sport, that's all. You'd better be ready."

"Will you be?"

Ramona laughed. "Don't worry about me. I'm all in. Shoot, I even practiced a little bit last night. I've got moves I never knew I had. Now all I need is a badass name."

<Click>

Willa Mae needed a moment to regain her equilibrium. Ramona Dorn's sudden confidence, and her eagerness to risk life and limb on a Derby track, left the rural gardener rattled and confused.

Surely, one night of practice couldn't have been enough to fire her up that much, she told herself.

Or could it?

~*~

Hildie had to wait for her shipment to arrive and booked a room in a motel near the mail service company. While not located in the best of neighborhoods, the establishment's manager eagerly accepted a cash payment and didn't bother to look at the information she jotted down on the check-in form.

She used her new-found free time to arrange for bus travel from Atlanta to Miami. Once there, she could enter the final stage of Phase Three. That would take a few weeks, after which time she planned to make one last visit to St. Charlotte before disappearing forever.

Chapter Nine

"The big divide in this country is not between Democrats and Republicans, or women and men, but between talkers and doers." – Thomas Sowell

Odell didn't often have to work late, but when duty called, he always stepped up, even if it meant he'd be unable to spend time with Ramona. He called her from his office, and after the usual pleasantries, he got to the point.

"Did anyone contact you about moving the garden club trophy out of the Convention Center?"

"No," she said. "Is there a problem?"

That's odd. "My nephew takes care of the place, and as you know, someone tried to break in the other night."

"Bubba's your nephew? I had no idea. I like him, and I feel terrible about the whole break-in thing," she said. "I'm just glad no one was hurt."

"Well, no one *we know*, anyway. It's just that he and I discussed moving it so he wouldn't have to stand guard over the darned thing. He's worried someone will steal it."

Ramona laughed. "You've seen it, right? Would you want it in your house?"

"And let it block the view of all my bowling trophies? No way."

"You're a bowler? Really?" She seemed genuinely surprised.

"No. The thing is, we've heard rumbling about someone in the area engaged in criminal activity, and it made me a little suspicious."

"Of the *trophy?*"

"Yes, actually. I don't have anything specific, and since this involves an ongoing investigation, I can't say much more than what I've already said."

"Whoa--an ongoing investigation? By your office?"

He smiled and shook his head from side to side even though she couldn't see him. "Anyway, Bubba asked me if I could store the trophy here at the station where he assumed it'd be safe. I said no, but in light of what I've heard, that may have been a mistake."

"It doesn't matter to me," Ramona said, "but Hildie was adamant about the trophy staying at the Convention Center where it would be visible at all our club meetings as well as the meetings of other organizations."

"Hmm. I suppose that's evidence of a certain amount of logic." He scratched his jaw. "At the very least, let's put an RFID tracker on it."

"A what?"

"RFID stands for Radio Frequency Identification

They're little computer chip thingies. Farmers used to attach 'em to the ears of their cattle to keep track of them. Now they're used for all sorts of things. We can hide one somewhere on the trophy, and if someone steals it, we can track it down easily. Bubba won't have to stay up all night on guard duty."

The following morning, Odell drove to the Convention Center and knocked on the locked front doors. An unaccompanied Bubba let him in.

"Holding down the fort all by yourself?" Odell asked.

"Yeah. Sheila went to get us some breakfast. I made coffee. Want some?"

Odell declined. "I can't stay long enough to drink it." He didn't bother to add that he'd once sampled what Bubba referred to as "coffee." It had taken a full twenty-four hours to recover. His heart went out to Sheila.

"Actually," he continued, "I just dropped by to tell you I've changed my mind about letting you store the garden club trophy at the station. There's plenty of room in our evidence storage area, and I'm the only one who has a key."

"Yeah, about that," Bubba began. "I've been giving it more thought."

"I imagine that break-in would help focus your thinking."

Bubba appeared untroubled. "*That* guy won't come back. Not after the knot Sheila put in his skull."

"On the other hand," Odell said, "he might want revenge. If there's one thing I've learned about criminals, especially the grab and go kind, they usually aren't very bright. Their brains generally stop long before they've thought about things like consequences. And motives?" His laugh contained no shred of humor. "Those are three for a dime."

"I dunno." Bubba shoved his hands in his pockets, hiked up his shoulders, and turned toward the end of the room where the drape-covered trophy stood. "Having it here sorta makes me important, ya know? Like, I'm trusted. Reliable. If we moved it, what would people think? It'd say just the opposite, wouldn't it? That I *can't* be trusted."

Odell gave him a smile he hoped wouldn't seem patronizing. "Or it might just convince them you've got their best interests at heart."

"Lemme think about it, okay?"

"Sure. And in the meantime, I'm going to hide a tracker on it. If someone gets past you, or breaks in while you're not around and carries it off, we'll be able to find it."

"That'd be awesome, Uncle Odell. Thank you."

After hiding the RFID chip among the baubles on the trophy, Odell walked back to his car. On the way he encountered Sheila carrying a paper bag from the town's lone doughnut shop along with a large, insulated, paper cup.

"Got your own coffee, I see," he said.

She grinned at him. "I never get fooled twice."

~*~

Two weeks passed before Ramona met with the general membership of the St. Charlotte Garden Club. As usual, the senior members clustered together near the front while everyone else sorted themselves largely by interest group. One could tell what those interests were based on an overheard word or two.

Constance DuBois, of course, swept through the

membership tirelessly, no doubt spreading whatever dubious intel she'd gathered. Ramona had no doubt Connie couldn't keep a secret if her lips were sewn shut.

"I'm pleased to announce that we've come to an agreement with our friends in the Charles County Club," she informed the gathering. "They've agreed to co-host our Roller Derby charity event. I know our club has a terrific history of serving St. Charlotte, and in many, many ways, but this time we're taking on a much bigger challenge than ever before."

"Here it comes," muttered Constance in a voice which carried across the room.

Ramona spelled out the details and wrapped up the presentation with a discussion of the timing. "We have just six weeks to get ready. That should work well for those who'd like to compete for the Henderson Horticultural Award."

"Do we know who all that is?" Constance asked. "And how much is the entry fee?"

"There's no entry fee," Ramona said. "We've been over that, Connie."

"Well, I still think—"

Ramona raised her voice and went on. "We didn't have much choice about the date for our Roller Derby match. The Atlanta and Savannah teams had to work it into their schedules, but they've been wonderfully helpful, and I just know it's going to be a great event."

"Starring you, of course," Constance said, her voice even more irritating than usual.

Ramona's shoulders drooped, but only briefly. She had no intention of letting the club's resident blowhard have her way. "As I recall, Connie, the last time we discussed this, you said there was no way you'd ever get up on skates. But if you really insist, I'll see what I can do to make that happen."

"Wait! I didn't— That's not—"

"See me after the meeting if you'd like to discuss this further," Ramona said. The increased chatter in the room confirmed her success at muzzling Constance. She waited until everyone settled down.

"For those of you interested in competing for the Henderson Award, you'll need to fill out a simple form which is attached to the rules. We'll have a small team of judges, none of whom are members of the sponsoring clubs. They've been working with local gardeners at the County Fair for years, so you'll probably recognize their names."

She rattled a sheet of paper containing the details, then read it out loud. "Karla Boyd, our wonderful newsletter editor, will include this information along with the contest rules and an entry form in the very next copy of *The Blossom*, so be on the lookout for it."

The rest of the usual club business was conducted at what seemed like light speed, and soon the Convention Center thinned out to just a handful of remaining club members, most of whom gathered around Ramona to thank her for her efforts.

It almost made the job worthwhile.

~*~

Still bothered by the confidence Ramona had voiced during their last phone call, Willa Mae began to wonder about her own sanity. If the roller-skating thing turned into the sort of train wreck she originally thought it would be, why had she gone along with the idea? And why had she turned herself into one of the engineers driving the locomotive?

But more than anything else, she couldn't wrap her

head around the change in Ramona Dorn. The woman actually sounded eager to compete. Somewhere along the way, Willa Mae had lost the initiative. That simply wasn't acceptable.

Which is why she called Ramona and arranged to meet her at the roller rink to do a little practice together. "I know we'll be competing against each other," she'd said, "but it can't hurt either of us to spend some time on wheels so we don't look like complete idiots."

Ramona had agreed, and they found a time and day to give it a try. That day had rolled around all too quickly, and Willa Mae found herself sitting beside Ramona as they laced up their rental skates.

"You know this is completely insane, right?"

Ramona nodded, then stuffed two sticks of Juicy Fruit gum in her mouth and chewed vigorously.

"You do that all the time?" Willa Mae asked.

"Nah," Ramona said, "but I haven't had time to buy a mouth guard." She chewed for a few moments, then unwrapped a third stick and shoved it in her mouth, too.

Willa Mae was appalled. "Is that... *normal* for you?"

She chewed for a while longer before responding. "Nope. I'm just trying to get myself in the mood. Besides, I have something that ought to help both of us."

Willa Mae frowned. She'd seen the shopping bag Ramona brought along, but she had no idea what might be in it.

"I can be so scattered at times. I should've given you these before we put our skates on." She handed Willa Mae a pair of thick knee pads.

"What? I—"

"These you can put on now," Ramona said as she dropped a pair of elbow pads in Willa Mae's lap.

"But—"

"And we'll both need one of these." The last items to leave the bag were a pair of helmets, one bright purple and one in neon green. "Can't leave our brains on the track, right?"

Willa Mae stared at her in surprise. "Did you buy these?"

Ramona shook her head. "The helmets are loaners; the pads are a gift from the Hip Hops. My friend, Jocelyn, made me promise I'd wear them while practicing. She wanted you to do the same." Ramona smiled and handed her the purple helmet. "Ya know, there's no reason why we can't be friends. Want some gum?"

Returning the smile, Willa Mae thanked her for the equipment and helped herself to the remains of the Juicy Fruit. "I'm a little embarrassed. I haven't done anything to earn your friendship. If anything, I've—"

"Forget it, whatever it is. We've got a chance to do something positive, together." Ramona removed her skates, slipped the knee pads into place, and put her skates back on. "You coming?"

"Yes. Absolutely!" Willa Mae scrambled to follow Ramona's lead.

"I'll see you out on the floor," Ramona said, as she worked her way across the carpeted area where skaters stored their belongings among scattered tables and chairs.

Willa Mae had been surprised to find the facility open during the day. She assumed most of the clientele consisted of kids, but they would normally be in school even though summer vacation loomed. And yet a number of people were cruising around and some were actually dancing. Most wore skates with a double row of wheels, like her rentals. But a handful wore skates with a single row of wheels. They were clearly speedsters, forsaking the graceful strides, turns, and twirls of the dancers, moves she wished she could emulate.

Ramona worked her way around the rink with neither the speed of the in-liners nor the grace of the dancers. She seemed to have some confidence but nowhere near the sort of command her attitude conveyed when they spoke on the phone. Willa Mae trudged across the carpet and stepped gingerly onto the hard surface of the skating rink.

Ramona rolled up beside her and stopped. "Wobbly?"

"Yeah," Willa Mae admitted. "Just a smidge. It's been a while since I last did this."

"It comes back pretty quick. At least, it did for me. C'mon," Ramona said. "Let's go. We'll go slow and stay near the edge for a few laps."

Willa Mae's confidence grew as they made their way around the arena. During their first three laps, neither faltered for more than a step or two, so Ramona suggested they try moving a little faster.

At one point, Ramona steered directly toward the tables and chairs. "I've gotta get rid of this gum. I'm drowning in saliva, and I can hardly breathe."

Willa Mae chuckled. She'd experienced much the same thing. After drinking some water, they headed back out onto the rink where one of the speeders slowed down and approached them.

"Nice helmets," he said. "I've got one that's similar, but I only wear it during competition, not practice. Are y'all derby girls?"

"Well, sorta," admitted Ramona. "But we're just getting started."

He smiled from one to the other. "I heard there would be a derby event around here. It's a great sport. My girlfriend loves it, but there aren't any teams nearby. Unless you're going to start one. Are you?"

Willa Mae offered a hurried summary, surprised at herself for opening up so easily to a stranger.

He introduced himself as Trent. "I'll be happy to give you a couple pointers," he said, "though it'd make more sense coming from Bethany. She's always wanted to be a jammer."

"Bethany's your girlfriend?"

"Yeah. She works here. I'd be happy to introduce you to her."

They spent the next half hour chasing after Trent, trying to emulate his style, bent forward at the waist, his legs moving smoothly from one side to the other. Though the idea was to catch Trent, their efforts became increasingly more competitive. Ramona moved faster through the straightaways, but Willa Mae managed tighter turns and would always catch up.

It went well, and they only crashed a couple times. Neither was willing to admit they'd been bruised, and by the time their hour was up, both had worked up a good sweat.

Trent introduced them to Bethany, and both Willa Mae and Ramona made an effort to talk her into joining one of their garden clubs. She wasn't interested, though she thought having gardeners sponsor a derby match amounted to the idea of the decade. Bethany offered to give them a few lessons, and both women signed up.

"I can't believe you tried to recruit that girl right out

from under me," Willa Mae said as they removed their skates and packed their gear.

Ramona grinned. "As I recall, you were trying to do the same thing."

"Well, yeah, but at least I asked her where she lived *before* I tried to strong arm her."

"No matter. I suspect it'll be a while before she's patient enough to watch plants grow."

"Same time, Saturday?" Willa Mae asked.

"Sure. But next time, you bring the chewing gum."

They parted company while visions of Double Bubble danced in Willa Mae's head.

~*~

"Where are you going?" Sheila asked.

"There's a fire. I just got the call."

Utterly puzzled, Sheila tilted her head. "Fire? Here?"

"No," Will said. "In town. St. Charlotte's version of the high rent district."

"So, what's that got to do with you?"

"I'm a fireman, sorta."

"Sorta?"

"Well, yeah. I'm a volunteer now, but I'm in the training program. They call me whenever there's a big blaze. Look, I'd love to stay here and chat, but—"

"But you've gotta go. I get it! Just..." she paused, "promise me you'll be careful."

He felt even closer to her than he had before. "I promise." He bent to give her a kiss.

"Do you think it'd be okay if I went with you?"

"To the fire? I guess it'd be all right. You'd have to promise to stay outta the way."

"I'd kinda like to see you in action," she said, her voice low and sexy.

He laughed. "I doubt they'll let me do much. Maybe drag a hose around or something. I haven't qualified for much else. C'mon, we've gotta get a move on."

Already dressed for the day, they both raced to Will's car. The drive to the site of the fire took little time, and they rolled to a stop well out of the way of the firefighters already working on the blaze.

"Have you got a helmet and coat and stuff?" Sheila asked.

"Not yet. But soon. Stay here, okay? I've gotta see what they need me to do."

Sheila watched him hurry away, straight toward the action which consisted of a large house on a generous, well-manicured lot. Smoke poured from the building, and she could see flames licking out from beneath the eaves at one end. It suddenly occurred to her that Will could easily find himself in a very dangerous situation. She'd never felt quite so unsettled. Even knowing he was in training, and that he didn't have the gear a normal fireman wore, her mind kept wandering into "what if" territory. *What if he did something stupid? What if he decided to be a hero? What if the roof caved in on him? What if—*

A commotion from the front of the house brought a much-needed distraction. A fire fighter in full regalia had a man slung over his shoulder as he emerged from the building. When they cleared the house and got closer, Sheila could see wisps of smoke drifting up from the man's clothing, though he clearly wasn't on fire.

The first responder stopped when he reached an ambulance and lowered his charge to a gurney which a pair of EMTs hustled toward him. The two attendants went to work immediately while the firefighter stepped away, coughing.

Sheila continued to watch as the two emergency techs soon stood up and looked at each other. One of them shook his head almost imperceptibly, but the message was unmistakable.

The shoulders of the fire fighter drooped as he turned and walked back to toward the building.

Sheila took it all in, but her thoughts remained on Will. Why would he want to become a part of something like this? *Volunteer* to participate in the aftermath of tragedy? What kind of person did that? Her thoughts continued to swirl, but gradually morphed into a question she'd never pondered, a question about herself.

~*~

"You're going to need a derby name," Odell told Ramona. He held his office phone in one hand and scrolled through a report that had just arrived from someone in the Georgia Bureau of Investigation. The information focused on Leonard Henderson, and it was anything but pleasant.

"I think I've got one," Ramona replied. "Wanna hear it?"

"Sure!"

"How's this? *Ram-moan-ah*. I'd spell it R-A-M then a hyphen, then M-O-N-A and another hyphen, and then A-H."

Odell chuckled. "It sounds ominous."

"It's supposed to, isn't it?"

"I guess," he said, "but I have a real hard time thinking of you in those terms."

"Wait'll you see me in my tight little derby shorts and stockings."

"Oh, darlin', believe me when I say I can't wait." He smiled at the thought.

Just then Minnie Harlow burst into his office. "Heads up, Odell. There's been a fire and what looks like a murder. You need to get on over to the Henderson place in The Hills."

He acknowledged the update with a look and a nod. "I've gotta run," Odell told Ramona. "But I'm serious about seeing you in your derby get-up. Tonight, maybe? If you're willing."

"We'll see," she said, dragging out the final syllable.

"Odell?" said Minnie, her voice insistent. "You need to get a move on."

He waved her off. "Okay then Miz *Ram-moan-ah*, I'll call you as soon as I can," he said and hung up the phone.

The drive to the Henderson home took ten minutes. Located in the most fashionable neighborhood in town, The Hills, a smoldering mansion sat amidst two acres of formerly well-tended grounds. A fire truck was just pulling away as Odell arrived.

Ren Taylor, head of the Fire Department stood beside a red SUV adorned with bright yellow and white SCFD signage.

"What's the story, Ren?" Odell asked.

"It's a complete mess," he said. "We got the call from

a neighbor who claims she saw two men leaving the place as smoke billowed out."

"Any idea who they were?"

Ren shook his head. "Not a clue. But they had to have been in there quite a while. The place looked as if someone had turned it upside down—stuff spread everywhere, and not just furniture. Drywall and paneling had been ripped off several walls, and the cupboards were torn down, too. I've never seen anything like it. But that's not the worst of it. There was a body."

"Any idea who it is?"

"We're pretty sure it's Leonard Henderson."

Odell squinted at him. "You're *pretty* sure? Was the body burned that badly?"

Ren shook his head, his face clouded. "It looked to me like someone beat him to death."

~*~

"I have a call for Mrs. Willa Mae Sundee," said a voice on the phone.

Willa Mae frowned at her phone. "I'm Will Mae Sundee. Who's—"

"Hold for Colonel Lovejoy."

Willa Mae frowned even harder. *Colonel Lovejoy?* She'd never heard of anyone by that name.

A high-pitched, male voice soon came on the line. "Good afternoon Mrs. Sundee. As the commanding officer of the 8th Armored, it's my duty to maintain decorum among our personnel. It's also my duty to see that our facilities are maintained at the highest possible state of readiness. There's no telling when this National Guard unit might be called up. That could occur at virtually any moment."

"General... What'd you say your name was again?"

"Lovejoy. And it's *Colonel* Lovejoy, not General. At least, not yet."

"I see. What happened to Colonel Miller? He was such a nice man. We got along really well."

Lovejoy prefaced his response with a gravely harrumph. "He's been reassigned. I don't know where, but I'm in command of the 108th now. The reason I'm calling—"

"Yeah, I wondered about that."

"I understand you and a Mrs. Dorn put in a facilities request."

"Which Colonel Miller approved. I have to tell you how excited our garden clubs are. This is such a wonderful opportunity. And the benefit to the children of Charles County is more than I can even guestimate. We're so thankful."

"I see," said Lovejoy. "Unfortunately, I must inform you that your facilities request came up for review, and it has been denied."

"When? Why? By who?"

"You mean 'by whom,' and that would be me."

"But—"

"Did you not hear me mention the word 'decorum' earlier? I should think that would be a sufficient explanation."

"Not for me, it isn't," Willa Mae said, making no effort to restrain the irritation in her voice. "Like I said, Colonel Miller already approved it. You can't just waltz in from the Pentagon, or Patagonia, or whatever hole you crawled out of and cancel our event."

"Actually, I can," he said. "And I did. You'll need to find another venue for your infantile derby, or whatever you call it. I won't have anything so ridiculous associated with the solemn role of the National Guard in the defense of this country. Good day madam."

<Click>

Though rarely at a loss for words, Willa Mae suddenly found herself in that state, compliments of Colonel Lovejoy. The condition didn't last long, and she conjured.

"Well now, you arrogant little twerp, we'll just see about that. I know people who know people."

At least, she *hoped* she knew people who knew people.

Chapter Ten

"Women are made to be loved, not understood."
– Oscar Wilde

"There's something I just don't understand," Sheila said to Will that evening. "Why would you risk yourself for someone you don't even know?"

"What d'ya mean?"

"Trying to be a fireman. That just seems to me to be... I dunno. Scary."

He nodded. "I s'pose someone could look at it that way, but I don't. You may think this is stupid, but I've always wanted to be a fireman."

"Seriously?"

"Yup. Ever since I was a kid. It just always seemed like a cool thing to do."

"Cool? Fighting fires?"

He grinned. "Yeah."

Sheila shook her head. "Is there anything else

you're involved in that I don't know about?"

"Well, there's the Guard. But that's not volunteer; it pays. It's only one weekend a month and a couple weeks in the summer. And you wouldn't believe what I get to do."

"The National Guard? Army stuff?"

"You got it. And I do have the uniforms for that, although we mostly just wear our fatigues."

"And you're *happy* about doing that?"

"Most of the time, sure. There are some great guys in my unit. A couple gals, too." He suddenly looked sheepish. "But they're just friends. I don't— I mean... I haven't tried to—"

"Relax," Sheila said. "You haven't known me long enough to cheat on me." She blew him a kiss. "Besides, I'm not in the least bit worried."

Will's smile lifted her heart. "So, you signed up to save not only the people here in St. Charlotte, but anywhere the government sends you?"

"I never thought about it that way, but yeah, pretty much."

She realized she had been holding her breath and took the opportunity to exhale. "How likely are you to be sent somewhere crazy? You know, like overseas."

"I have no idea. If they need armored personnel carriers somewhere, I guess they could send us. Does that bother you?"

"It bothers me that it doesn't bother *you*!"

Will chuckled. "Oh. Well, it's not really a big deal, although it might be kinda neat to go somewhere I've never been."

"Like some godforsaken desert?"

"I was thinkin' more like Hawaii."

Sheila groaned. "Will, sweetheart, they're never going to send the National Guard to Hawaii. Not unless some other country invades it first."

His eyebrows drew down in concern. "Who'd do that? China, maybe?"

She shook her head. "What? I don't know! How much longer do you have in your current enlistment?"

"I'll be done this fall, but they want me to re-up."

"Don't!" she said, her voice rising.

"Why not? It's easy money."

"It's easy right up until they send you to Africanistan or some other nasty place. Baby, I couldn't stand that." She reached for him and hugged him tight.

"Seriously?" he asked, pulling away slightly. "You're worried? About *me*?"

"Yeah," she said, blinking away a tear. "I am."

~*~

When her phone rang, Ramona glanced reflexively at the number. The volume of sales calls and scams had escalated over the past few years, and like many people, she opted not to answer calls from numbers she didn't recognize. This call, however originated in area code 305, which she thought was somewhere in Florida. And, since several garden club members had retired there recently, she decided to take a chance and answer it. One never knew.

"H'lo?"

"Ramona. It's me, Hildie. Are you alone? If not, don'

say my name."

Hildie? Holy moly! You're alive? "Hildie!" she exclaimed. "Oh, dang. Sorry."

"Are you alone?"

"Yes," Ramona said quickly. "I'm alone."

"Thank goodness."

Ramona needed a moment to recover from her shock. "Where the heck are you? *How are you?* My God, I thought—we *all* thought—you were... well... dead."

"Good."

"*Good?*"

"It's best for everyone to keep thinking that," Hildie said.

"What? Why? I don't understand. Hildie, where the hell are you?"

"I'm sorry, but I just can't tell you. Suffice it to say I'm safe for the time being."

"For the time being? Please, stop. I don't understand any of this. I need to know—"

"Listen to me, Ramona. There's very little you need to know other than this: my husband is a criminal. I have no idea how long he's been involved with the mob or whoever it is that has their claws in him."

"I thought he was an accountant," Ramona said.

"He used to be. The man I married was, anyway. I don't know when he lost his way. I have my suspicions, however. A few years ago, he started buying up all these little companies. I didn't think much of it at the time; I just assumed he knew what he was doing. Not long after that it seemed like we had more than enough money for anything we wanted.' She paused for a breath.

"And then we moved. I think I've told you how much I loved our old home, but he insisted we needed something bigger. He bought a huge house with a gigantic lot and paid for just about anything I asked for—a water feature, statuary, shrubbery from the most exclusive nurseries. Nothing seemed too expensive."

"So, what makes you think he was involved in something illegal?" Ramona asked.

"He wouldn't tell me any of the details of his businesses. Men would show up at odd hours with huge bundles. Leonard stored them in the garage, but wouldn't let me near them. Over the course of a few days they would disappear, and he refused to tell me what they contained."

"Drugs, you think?"

"Money. Cash he moved through the accounts of all the little businesses he owned in order to hide it from the government."

Ramona couldn't believe what she was hearing. "How do you know all this?"

"Because I finally got a look at his books. It didn't take long to figure it out. I asked him about it, and he denied it at first. Then he told me the truth. He told me about his escape plan and how he figured to leave the life, how we'd both be safe and comfortable."

"I still don't—"

"Let me finish, Ramona. And please understand, I'm sharing this with the utmost secrecy. I'm counting on you not to say a word about any of this to anyone."

"But... why me?"

"I'll get to that. The final straw was when I realized Leonard had no intention of including me in his so-called 'escape plan.' It turns out he has a girlfriend, a much younger woman than me, and all along he intended to take her with him. He was going to leave me behind to face the bad guys all alone."

Ramona couldn't believe her ears. "What a... a bastard!"

"My thoughts exactly," Hildie said. "So, I worked out my own escape plan."

"And that's why you can't tell me where you are?"

"Certainly not on the phone, anyway. But there's a little more. I made a copy of Leonard's records for the past year. Some of the names are in code, but most of them are fairly easy to figure out. If I could do it, I know the FBI could."

"Where is this list?" Ramona asked.

"It's hidden in a safe place along with the last of my escape money. I intend to return to St. Charlotte and retrieve everything, but if something goes wrong, if I can't get back or—God forbid—the mob gets to me, I want someone else to know about it. That someone is you."

"*Me?* Why? Oh God, Hildie, I don't know if—"

"I trust you, Ramona. More than anyone else I know."

"I hope I'm worthy of that trust," Ramona said, dubiously. "But in case you hadn't heard, I need to tell you about Leonard."

"He's been arrested, hasn't he," Hildie said, without a hint of a question in her voice.

"No," Ramona said. "He's been... murdered."

Hildie's sharp intake of breath told her the news hadn't reached her. "I'm sorry, Hildie. The article in the paper didn't have many details. No one seems to know who did it but the police—"

"I know who did it," Hildie said. "And I know why." She paused for a moment before continuing. "Can't say I'm surprised, or upset, for that matter. It's exactly what Leonard intended for me."

~*~

Odell sat at his desk reviewing a number of reports turned in by his deputies. Several small firms in the area had been hit by a pair of thugs who sounded suspiciously like the two men seen leaving the Henderson house shortly before it caught fire.

The thing that struck him as odd was the fact that no one from the businesses involved had filed complaints or asked for help. The reports all originated from people who witnessed the disturbances from a distance. Not a single victim had reached out to his office or the state patrol.

An uneasy feeling came over him as he reviewed the notes from his staff and mulled over reports from the Georgia Bureau of Investigation.

What made the whole situation more ominous was the disappearance of Leonard Henderson's wife. Just because Henderson held a memorial service for her didn't mean her body had been found. As far as Odell knew, it hadn't been.

Ramona had been a friend of the woman. He prayed she wasn't somehow involved in what was looking very much like a major crime scheme.

~*~

"We've got a problem," Willa Mae told Ramona at the skating rink. "We may not need to practice anymore."

"What do you mean?" demanded Ramona. "What are

you talking about?"

Willa Mae told her about Colonel Lovejoy and his decision to cancel their request to use the National Guard facility.

"He can't do that!" Ramona said. "Can he?"

"That's *exactly* what he did. Called me up and told me himself, the pompous little windbag. I got in touch with some of the girls in my club to see if any of them knew someone who might have some pull with the National Guard."

"And?"

"I came up empty. I'm hoping you know someone."

"Me?" Ramona whistled a worried note. "I can ask around."

"Would you, please? After everything we've done to get this darn thing organized, I'd hate to see it blow up in our faces."

"I agree."

"Oh," said Willa Mae. "One other thing: I've gotten a couple calls from club members. There are several who've signed up to compete for the trophy."

"Actually," Ramona said, "there are exactly five, same as from our club. Oh, and one independent."

"Have any of your club members mentioned sabotage to you?"

"Wait. Did you say *sabotage*?"

~*~

Hildie kept a careful eye on her expenditures. What cash she had left would have to sustain her through her plastic surgery and the time it would take to heal. She'd done a dozen estimates and knew that if she didn't go overboard, the funds would last.

The call to Ramona may or may not have been a mistake. She prayed she had judged Ramona's character properly. If so, she'd keep the news of Hildie's survival a secret along with everything else. There would come a time when the whole sordid story could come out, but not before Hildie secured her future, preferably in a country that didn't have an extradition treaty with the United States.

"Miss Smith?" asked an attractive woman in surgical scrubs. "We're ready for you."

Hildie smiled back at the woman. "I sure hope I'm not making a mistake."

"You'll be fine. Doctor Cornblooth is a true genius, and you're going to love your new look."

"He said it would take several weeks to heal completely," Hildie said. "Will I look hideous in the interim?"

"There's going to be some bruising, swelling, and discoloration. There's no way around that. But the people in the recovery center where you'll be staying are completely used to it. They'll make you feel wonderful, and the time will slip by faster than you can imagine. Before you know it, you'll be going out into the world looking at least ten years younger if not more. I hope you're ready to start dating again!"

Nothing could have appealed to Hildie less at that moment. For her, the essential thing was to look *different*. If Dr. Cornblooth made her look younger, too, that would simply be a bonus. Vanity had nothing to do with her surgery; it was all about survival. By now, Leonard's hoodlum pals should have discovered some of their cash was missing, and it wouldn't take a genius to figure out who had it.

~*~

Sheila knew her body well. She never guessed about things like her period; it occurred like clockwork, almost as if it were set by the same atomic gizmo all the governments in the world relied on. And she was never late.

Until now.

But had her diaphragm failed when she was with Will or Monty? The memory of her encounter with the latter still gave her the shakes. It couldn't have been Monty, she reasoned. God would never play that nasty a trick on anyone.

Blaming her condition on anyone other than herself, she knew, was a waste of time. She'd taken two lovers, one of whom she'd fallen for. How would he react to the idea of being a parent? For that matter, how did she feel about it?

For reasons she couldn't begin to explain, much less understand, she felt remarkably calm. But then, she was only a few days late. No more than a week at most.

I'm overreacting. They say our bodies change as we get older. Older? I'm only thirty-two! That's not old. That's….

That's not the point. I'm pregnant.

Maybe.

~*~

Ramona talked most of the executive committee and some of the senior members into attending an emergency meeting. Few were happy about it, but even fewer objected once they understood the reason why she'd called it.

"As I told most of you on the phone, there's been a major roadblock dumped in front of our derby effort to fund the playground for special needs children. The action was taken by Col. Quincy Lovejoy, the new commander at the

National Guard armory."

Karla Boyd raised her hand, and spoke when Ramona acknowledged her. "I don't understand how anyone could stand in the way of our building a playground for such deserving kids. Did this Col. Lovehandles understand why we were doing it?"

"I don't know," Ramona said. "I didn't get the call. It went to Willa Mae Sundee, she's president of the rural club."

Another member spoke up. "What happened to Col. Miller? I thought he was in charge over there."

"I asked the same question," Ramona said. "I'm told he was reassigned."

A trio of senior members near the back of the room conducted a brief but hushed huddle then went quiet and turned their attention back to their President.

"I'm hoping someone in this room knows the new base commander well enough to explain things to him in a way he'll understand. Willa Mae gave me the impression he didn't think a roller derby was dignified enough to take place in the assembly area of the armory."

Annabelle Knox, one of the three caucusing seniors, got slowly to her feet and stretched a bit before she spoke. "Tell me this man's name again."

Ramona spelled it out for her.

"I'd appreciate it if you jotted that down for me." She cleared her throat and continued, "My husband dropped me off for this morning on his way to a ROMEO breakfast."

"Romeo?"

She smiled. "That'd be 'Real Old Men Eatin' Out.' He's been a member for a long, long time. Anyway, he has some good friends in that group, and I've met a few of their wives. Nice ladies, most of 'em." She paused as if ruminating on her acquaintances.

"And?" Ramona prompted.

"Oh, right. Well, as I recall, one of those ladies is the Governor's sister, and I'm pretty sure she helped him with his campaign. Best of all, she's a gardener. We've talked a few times about roses; she loves roses. Anyway, I imagine she could put in a good word for us."

"Bless you, Annabelle," Ramona said. "Will you please let me know what she says?"

Annabelle grinned. "I don't mind at all, dear. But there's a good chance you'll hear directly from Lieutenant Lovehandles himself. 'Course, by then, he might be a private."

~*~

"Sheila," Bubba said, trying to sound more sure of himself than he felt, "I think we need to talk about your skin-the-trophy idea."

She chuckled. "What's on your mind?"

"It's kind of a good news/bad news thing. Chief Taylor told me the county would pay for me to go through some training courses at the Fire Academy, and if I did well enough, they'd offer me a paid job. I'd be a real firefighter."

He could tell the idea didn't thrill her, but she put on a happy face anyway.

"That's great!" she said. "You should be glad."

"I am, sorta. But it means I'll have to spend some time away from here, away from... us. And so, I thought maybe I should—"

"Stop right there, mister." She put a finger on his lips. "This is something you've wanted all your life. Don't you dare back out."

"I may not have a choice," he said. "I'm in charge of this dumb conference center. Who's going to take care of it while I'm gone?"

"How hard can it be?"

He felt distinctly sheepish. "Thing is," he said, lowering his head, "there's a lot more to it than I've done. The clean-up is no big deal, and I take care of the grounds—you know, mowing and stuff."

"So, what else is there?"

"I'm supposed to go out and show the place to new users. Sign up new groups to use it." His shoulders drooped. "I'm terrible at that kinda stuff."

Sheila reached for his chin, gently lifting it so he'd look in her eyes. "It's salesmanship, not magic. It just takes a little time to learn. I can teach you."

"You would?"

"Of course! But I'm wondering what all this has to do with our making some adjustments to the trophy."

Bubba swallowed hard, hoping she wouldn't be upset or disappointed. "I think we shouldn't do it. We've got something going, and... I dunno. Things seem to be really turning around for me now. If we got caught, we'd lose everything." He recalled the chat he'd had about the stupidity of thieves with his uncle Odell, yet another person in his life he didn't want to disappoint.

To his relief, Sheila smiled. "I know we haven't been together very long, and you really don't know much about me."

"I know I love you!"

"And I feel the same way about you. I had no idea that would change me, change the way I think and act. I've been on my own for a long time, Will. Too long, I suppose. I never had to care about someone else, even when I was a kid."

It sounded all too familiar to him. "I get it."

"When I see what you want to do with your life, it makes me ashamed of my own."

Bubba waved his hand at the Convention Center. "Yeah, look at me, the king of all this." He shook his head. "I haven't accomplished anything."

"Oh yeah, you have," she said. "You changed me. That's an accomplishment. You want to help people and make a difference. I've always been content to rip people off and sneak away. I could never be like you. I don't have the guts."

"I don't feel brave at all," he said. "But maybe it's something we could work on, together. You know, when you're not teaching me how to be a salesman."

She kissed him.

~*~

"I don't know why we keep doing this," said Willa Mae when she and Ramona took a break from skate practice. The rink held more skaters than usual since school let out for the summer, and the two adults frequently had to make emergency maneuvers in order to avoid crashing into kids, many of whom were much slower and more tentative in their efforts to stay upright. Both of the garden clubbers had moved well past that stage, each determined to outskate the other, but neither able to claim superiority.

"We keep skating 'cause it's fun," Ramona said, "and it's the only exercise we get."

"True," admitted Willa Mae, "but I was referring to our being banned from the armory by Captain Killjoy."

"It's only been three weeks since my friend Annabelle said she'd get in touch with the governor's sister." Ramona took a swig from her water bottle. "I'll give her a call and see if she's heard anything."

"What're we going to do if we can't use the armory?" Willa Mae followed Ramona's example and took a long pull on her own water bottle.

"There's the high school gym," Ramona said.

Willa Mae frowned. "St. Charlotte High or Charles County High?"

"I don't care."

"Doesn't matter. I doubt we'd be able to talk either school into letting us in. Those gym floors are hardwood. They don't allow people in street shoes to walk on them. You think they'd let us roller skate on 'em?"

"Probably not," Ramona said. "I told Odell—"

"Your boyfriend? The police chief?"

"Sheriff."

"Right," Willa Mae said with an eyeroll.

"Anyway, he suggested we might be able to use the firehouse. They've got room for two big trucks. All they'd have to do is pull them out on the street."

Willa Mae shook her head. "There'd be no space for spectators, and that's what it's all about, right? The more people who attend, the more money we collect for the playground."

"There's always the fairgrounds," Ramona said.

"I thought of that," Willa Mae commented between sips of water, "and looked into it. In fact, I checked with the guy who runs the place, and he said we were welcome to use it. The problem is, there's no paved area big enough. Most of the seating is in the arena, and it's designed for livestock and rodeos, not roller skaters."

Ramona lowered her head. "So, unless we close off a section of I-75 and borrow some bleachers from the baseball fields for viewers, we're sunk."

"Maybe not," Willa Mae said. "If we absolutely had to, we could set up in that big parking lot in front of the Piggly Wiggly. It's never full. We'd just have to pray for decent weather."

Ramona grinned at her. "That's a great idea! We need to check with the grocery and—"

"Already done," Willa Mae said, trying not to sound smug. "They offered to co-sponsor the event in hopes of getting some good publicity. Oh, yeah, and they asked that we have some police on site." She squinted at her companion. "That shouldn't be a problem, should it?"

"I can call in a favor or two," Ramona said, still grinning.

"I'll just bet you can." Willa Mae set her water bottle aside. "Do you remember a while back I mentioned sabotage?"

"Yeah, but I wasn't sure what you meant."

"All five of my club members who signed up for the contest claim someone has poisoned parts of their their gardens."

"You're kidding, right?" Ramona appeared shocked.

"Nope. I was wondering if any of *your* club members have said anything."

"Not a one."

Willa Mae was unable to keep from pursing her lips. "Can I say I'm not surprised?"

"Wait. You don't think my club has anything to do with it, do you?"

"I think the facts speak for themselves."

"I promise you, I'll look into it," Ramona said. "How much damage has been done?"

"It varies. My friend Kathy had her entire rose bed wiped out. She contacted a friend at the Agricultural Extension Office and provided samples. She was told someone had sprayed them with a powerful herbicide. They died pretty fast."

"That's terrible! I can't imagine—"

"Maybe you could get your boyfriend to investigate."

"Count on it."

"Meanwhile," Willa Mae said, "we'll look after our own. The club bought some motion-activated cameras to catch whoever might come back and try something else, although to be honest, it's probably too late; the damage has already been done."

"Were the cameras very expensive?" Ramona held up her hand. "It doesn't matter. I'll make sure we do the same thing."

"Do me one more favor," Willa Mae said. "Set the cameras up yourself, or let your boyfriend do it. Don't tell anyone else, especially not the other contestants."

"Good idea," Ramona said. "I'll set 'em up myself. I'm sure Odell will help me."

Chapter Eleven

"It may be a cock that crows, but it's the hen that lays the eggs." – Margaret Thatcher

Slightly distracted when her cell rang, Ramona answered without thinking. "H'lo?"

"I have a call for Mrs. Ramona Dorn," said a flat voice on the phone.

Ramona exhaled wearily. "Speaking."

"Hold for Colonel Lovejoy."

And instantly Ramona found herself off-task, drumming her fingers, and waiting for a new load of verbal fertilizer from the head of the local Guard post. After what she'd heard from Willa Mae about the conversation she'd had with him, Ramona didn't hold out much hope. Making matters worse, her second call to Annabelle Knox had not gone well. The woman only vaguely recalled discussing the matter at the garden club meeting. When Ramona refreshed her memory, Annabelle promised to follow through.

"Mrs. Dorn?" a man's voice asked, but rather than wait for a response, he cleared his throat twice.

Ramona waited for a break in the rumble. "Yes, I'm still here, but you don't sound well at all, Major."

"It's *Colonel* Lovejoy." He cleared his throat again, though it didn't lower the pitch of his voice; he still sounded like an alto. "Now, it seems there's been... Uh... So, the reason I called..." His voice drifted into a brief silence as if he were gathering strength for a charge. "See here, Mrs. Dorn, have you any idea how important it is for people to go through the proper channels? The safety and security of our entire country absolutely depend on a rigorous adherence to protocol."

"Who knew?" Ramona said sweetly, sensing a clumsy retreat by the undeniably misnamed officer. "You make it sound so... profound. And yet, in times of emergencies—"

"Your ridiculous roller-skating party hardly qualifies as an emergency."

"To you, perhaps," she said. "But cancelling our event definitely created an emergency for us. Is that why you're calling? Have you had a change of heart?"

"Certainly not. My personal feelings haven't changed one iota," Lovejoy said. "However, it seems there are other factors to be considered now, and it appears there's been a misunderstanding."

"A *misunderstanding?* Oh, I doubt that. From what I've heard, you were quite clear about the issue when you contacted my co-chair," Ramona said. "We got your message loud and clear."

"I'm trying to be diplomatic here," Lovejoy said. "I didn't call to argue over the particulars."

"Well then," Ramona suggested, "you might want to start with an apology."

Though she couldn't see his face, and had no idea what he looked like, she thought she could hear him grind his teeth and imagined a uniformed adult experiencing the kind of emotional trauma more commonly expressed by four-year-olds in need of a nap.

"After a further review, your request to use the Army National Guard armory for a charity event has been approved."

Ramona smiled. "See? That wasn't so hard, was it?"

Lovejoy's response consisted of more throat clearing.

"You really need to have that checked," she said. "And thank you for calling with the news."

Ramona couldn't wait to ring up Willa Mae and deliver the update. Why Lovejoy had called her instead of his original contact remained a mystery, but the turn-around amounted to news she had to share. Yet, before she could dial Willa Mae's number, she received a call from Annabelle.

"I don't know what you told the Governor's sister, Annabelle, but it sure worked."

"Good," said the long-time club member. "I'm happy I could help, even if... You know, some days I'm a little forgetful, and I don't know why. Probably not enough greens in my diet."

Ramona tried not to chuckle. "I'm sure that's it. Was there something else you needed to tell me?"

"Actually, there is," she said. "And I hope you won't think I'm being silly."

"You, silly? Never," said Ramona. "Please, fire away!"

"Some of the ladies were telling me they wished they could somehow participate in the fund raiser. We're all way too old to skate, but surely there's something we could do."

"After all the work you've already put into this club?" Ramona gave her a good-natured laugh. "We should just be thanking all of you for your years of service. And maybe giving you a discount on front row seats."

"That would be nice, but we had something else in mind."

"Really?"

"What would you think of having some cheerleaders on hand. You know, for both teams. Maybe help keep the crowd interested?"

"I think that would be fun," Ramona said. "Were you planning on contacting the high schools? I'll bet—"

"No," Maybell said. "Nothing like that. My friends and I would like to do it ourselves. And I'll bet some of the ladies from the other club would be interested, too."

~*~

"I can't believe we're doing this," Odell said as he and Ramona settled down in the shadow of some trees and waited for the sun to set. "What if someone sees us?"

"Come on, Odell. You're the Sheriff. Just tell them you're investigating something."

"Like what?"

"I dunno. A neighborhood disturbance or a lost dog."

"We don't look for lost animals." He paused for a moment. "Actually, that's not completely accurate. We've had to send out patrol cars from time to time when a cow or two get loose. That's kinda the same thing, isn't it?"

Ramona gave his shoulder a light punch. "Use your imagination."

"Yeah, okay. I'll think of something."

"You know what really scares me?" Ramona asked.

"That *you'll* get caught out here?" He laughed. "I'd have to take you in, cuffs and all."

"I'm serious. What if we find out it's a club member who's been killing the flowers? That'd be awful."

"So? You kick them out of the club. That's all. See if anybody wants to press charges."

"I guess." Another few minutes passed, but the sun hadn't seemed to move. "Y'know," she said, "we could be out here for quite a while."

"No kidding. How many cameras do we need to set up?"

"Five in all."

"In the dark."

"Yep."

"Without getting caught."

Ramona reached for the open collar of his shirt with both hands and grabbed hold. "Is my big, brave lawman turning into a scaredy cat?"

"Nonsense, woman. It's just—"

"Oh, dear Lord. Are you going to deliver a bucket of pomp and protocol like Col. Killjoy?"

"What? No!" Odell liberated his shirt front and straightened it. "Well, not exactly. It's just—"

"Go ahead. Ruin my evening."

169

He hugged her. "I have a position of authority. People expect me to, you know, represent law and order."

"And you are!"

"By skulking around in the dark?"

"For one thing, it's not dark yet. And I don't intend to skulk. I don't even know what that would look like. Besides, we're trying to solve a crime, or at least, a potential crime."

"Poisoning someone's flowers isn't likely to land a perp on the Most Wanted List."

"True, but at the very least, we could get 'em for trespassing."

"And," he added, "destruction of property. But a good lawyer would have 'em out on the street in no time."

"If nothing else, we'd know who's behind it," Ramona said. "That may not be a big deal for you, but for my club, it's huge."

Odell gave in, as they both had known he would from the start. "So, how do you propose we pass the time until dark?" He gave her another squeeze. "We could crawl into the back of my car and—"

"Why, Sherriff Odum, you lecherous thing! How dare you insinuate that a lady of my standing in the community would even think of entertaining such a thought. I'm—"

"Get in the car, girl."

She giggled a bit, then added, "Race ya!"

~*~

Hildie looked at herself in the mirror, still stunned by the visage which greeted her. It simply wasn't... *her*.

She turned her head from side to side and examined

the faint scarring which the surgeon assured her would fade to almost nothing. Though the procedure hadn't done anything drastic, the changes were sufficient to make her look similar to the old Hildie, but definitely not the same. Modifications to her hair color and style would help, too.

All of which would be a huge help when she fully assumed her new identity. At first, she'd had no idea how to go about finding someone to help her create a past that would escape scrutiny. Not that she needed something as foolproof as a spy for the CIA, but she definitely needed something good enough to fool the mob until she slipped out of the country. Eventually, however, as a result of careful inquiries, she'd found someone to help her, a young woman named Eva Grant. At least, that's the name she *claimed* was hers. For all Hildie knew, "Eva" was merely one of several identities.

Hildie would be quite happy with just one.

"You're going to need to familiarize yourself with this background information," Eva told her as she handed over a thumb drive.

Hildie instantly recognized the device. She'd used one to record the copies she'd made of Leonard's records. She responded with a small snort of laughter. "Guess I need to get a laptop somewhere."

"They're pretty cheap nowadays," Eva said, "unless you want to be a competitive gamer or something."

"Nope, I just want to be..." She paused. "I don't even know what my new name is."

"It's Alexis Rae. The identity is real, although the original Alexis Rae is no longer with us."

Hildie looked up in shock. "Wha—"

"She passed away a year ago while training to climb a

mountain in Tibet or some crazy place. Sadly, for her, but good for you, she no longer had any family. She was born a couple years after you were, so congratulations; you get to re-celebrate some birthdays. All the details are in files on the thumb drive. You'll be able to get an official copy of Alexi Rae's birth certificate and use it to get yourself a new driver' license and passport. That should allow you to go just about anywhere. Just... You know; don't go overboard. Stay in the background. Don't start a second career in Hollywood o anything."

Relieved, though slightly unsettled knowing the sad particulars of the woman whose identity she was stealing Hildie tried to laugh at Eva's joke. "I'm a little old for stage and screen, don't you think?"

Eva smiled. "I dunno. You look pretty good to me. And on second thought, maybe a supporting role would by okay.

"Thank you," Hildie said. "You've saved my life." She handed her an envelope containing a significant chunk of her remaining cash which the younger woman promptly counted

"We're good," Eva said. "Have a nice life, Lexi."

"Lexi?"

"Sure. It fits, doesn't it?" Eva grinned, then turned and walked away.

Lexi. Hildie rolled her new name around in her head then said it out loud several times. *I like it.*

It was finally time to return to St. Charlotte and execute the last phase of her escape plan.

~*~

Willa Mae returned home tired, sore in several places and yet proud of herself. She and Ramona had met with their respective teams in what the derby girls called a scrimmage, something Willa Mae had thought was reserved for football. The teams met at a strip mall that ceased construction when the real estate market collapsed. It was in Macon, a spot roughly halfway between Atlanta and Savannah, so neither team had to drive too far. In no time at all they outlined a track using bright yellow duct tape.

The workout had been grueling. Even though she and Ramona had tried to ramp up their practice sessions, zipping around a track with women who really knew what they were doing proved intimidating. At least at first. But gradually, both garden club leaders pushed harder, bumped shoulders and hips, and worked every advantage they could find.

The veteran skaters, all at least a few years younger, complimented the newcomers. Willa Mae assumed they were just being nice, but their comments made her feel good nonetheless.

She had just settled down to a well-deserved glass of Chardonnay when Ramona called.

"We've got film of the jerk who's been killing the flowers."

"That's great! Do you know his name?"

"Unfortunately, no," Ramona said, "but I will show the video at our meeting tomorrow. Hopefully, someone will recognize him."

"Please let me know what you find out."

"Absolutely."

"Oh, and Ramona? I had fun today, but I sure hope my bumps and bruises clear up before our event."

"I'm with you. By the way, you wouldn't know anyone

with a hot tub, would ya?"

Willa Mae grinned as she stared out the window toward the six-person tub her husband had purchased as a family Christmas present. "As a matter of fact, I do. Grab a swimsuit and hop on down. I'll whip up something to snack on."

"You're a life saver," Ramona said. "I'll bring wine."

~*~

Sheila couldn't quite put her finger on her feelings as she attended the garden club meeting in the Conference Center. It was the first one she'd been to without an ulterior motive, and she found it odd.

The club's President, Ramona Dorn, was going through the plans for the big charity event they would stage at the nearby National Guard armory. When Sheila first heard about the event, she worried they might try to talk her into being a competitor. Not because she claimed any great skill on roller skates, but simply because she was a good bit younger than most of the other club members.

Fortunately, nothing had come of that. But something new did grab her attention—Ramona's comments about sportsmanship.

"As much as I hate to do it," President Dorn said, "I must bring up a subject which troubles me. In fact, it's kept me awake nights. A few of you may already be aware of this, but I recently learned that someone involved with our contest has been cheating. Someone has been spraying a powerful herbicide on flowers in the gardens of several people who entered the Henderson Horticultural Contest."

A collective gasp went up among the attendees, Sheila included. It was one thing to be sneaky about winning a contest, but killing the competition had never been her *modus operandi,* and she couldn't imagine anyone who might do such a thing. Even for someone like her, whose morals could be counted on a single digit, murder—even of plants—was just plain wrong.

Ramona went on to explain how, with the assistance of the Charles County Sheriff's Department, motion-activated cameras had been secretly installed on all the properties of contestants whose gardens had not already been compromised.

"It was my fervent prayer," she said, "that no one connected with either of the sponsoring clubs had anything to do with such an underhanded and criminal act."

She pointed to a projector screen set up at the front of the room and signaled for Karla Boyd to dim the room's lights and start the video. In short order, the oddly illuminated, night-vision film revealed a man sneaking into the backyard of a home and spraying something on several of the flowering plants he found there.

"Can anyone identify that guy?" Ramona asked at the end of the short clip.

Sheila held her breath. *Could it be?* She raised her hand, and when recognized, asked to have the clip run again. She watched even more carefully the second time, and at the conclusion, she felt quite sure she knew exactly who it was.

After raising her hand once again, Sheila was called on. "You want me to just say his name in front of everyone? Right here? I mean, what if I'm wrong? What if the man I identify has an alibi?"

Ramona looked grim. "If you know something, now's the time to speak up."

Sheila swallowed. She hadn't ratted on anyone since she was in the second grade, and then only because it meant she wouldn't get into deeper trouble herself. "Okay," she said, "I'm pretty sure I know who it is."

"*Pretty* sure?" Ramona asked.

"Well, no." Sheila straightened up in her seat. "I'm absolutely certain I know who it is."

~*~

Sitting at his desk with a rare third cup of coffee in hand, Odell reviewed two new reports which had been filed overnight. Both involved small business break-ins, which was troubling, but not terribly unusual. Petty crime never seemed to end, no matter how well the overall economy performed.

What made these crimes stand out was the apparent lack of concern by the people who ran the businesses, just as had happened before. This time, a florist and a tune-up shop had been ransacked, and their storage areas destroyed. And yet, if not for concerned neighbors, the crimes may never have been called in.

Odell tightened his fists in frustration. Obviously someone capable of instilling great fear had used it to find whatever they'd lost. The circumstances screamed organized crime, but he was reluctant to believe St. Charlotte offered a lucrative enough environment for that. And yet just such a connection went a long way toward explaining the break-in and Leonard Henderson's murder. He'd been assured the GBI was working on the case, but knowing that didn't make him any more patient.

Odell had asked the county clerk to find out what business licenses were held in Leonard's name or that of his accounting firm. Not surprisingly, all the shops destroyed in the past couple weeks had been connected to him.

It required no great genius to determine that Leonard Henderson had been laundering money for someone. At some point, things must have gone sour, which probably led to the disappearance of Leonard's wife, Hildegard. In a matter of weeks, Leonard was beaten to death, his home was ransacked and burned, and the companies he'd been involved with had all been plundered. In all likelihood, whoever was behind it still hadn't found what they were looking for, otherwise the looting would have ended.

Very little forensic evidence had been recovered, and the eyewitness accounts of the two men responsible didn't offer much help. Odell felt hamstrung, unsure what to do and worried about what might come next, if anything at all.

No, he decided. There would be *something*.

Ramona couldn't wait to chat with the young woman who claimed to know the man in the video, but several club members intervened before she could reach her. Much to her surprise, Constance DuBois wasn't among them. Instead, a small but vocal delegation which included Annabelle Knox, presented itself.

"We need to know what our team colors are," said one.

"There's not much time left to put in an order for pompoms," said another.

"And we've got to make our uniforms!" exclaimed a third.

Ramona hadn't seen so much excitement amongst the senior members since a local coffee shop instituted half-price Tuesdays for anyone over sixty-five. "Wow! Y'all are really getting into this. I— I don't know what to say."

"You could start by telling us what our team colors

are. Or, can we just choose them?" Annabelle had a look on her face that reminded Ramona of long-ago Christmas mornings when her son Donny would ask if Santa had come.

"Our girls will be wearing green, really bright, neon green. And black. And maybe some white, too." Ramona smiled at them. "There'll be lots of makeup, and some. unusual hair styles."

"Oh, we know," said Annabelle. "I got my granddaughter to look up some videos for us on her computer. There's no way we would try to match *them!* We'll be going for a more traditional look."

Ramona grinned in relief. "So, anything else?"

"No, that's it," Annabelle said. "Neon green. That's all we needed to know, except—"

"What?" Ramona asked.

"Do you suppose anyone makes a plaid in those colors?"

"Let's go find out," suggested another. "I'll drive!"

By the time they'd moved out of her way, Ramona lost sight of the younger woman she'd been so eager to reach. Fortunately, she spotted her near a door leading to the interior of the building. She waved and called out to get her attention, and the woman turned, acknowledging her.

"I know we've met," Ramona said, "but frankly, I'm terrible with names. Please tell me yours again."

The younger woman chuckled. "I'm terrible at names too. I'm Sheila Moran."

"I'm Ramona," she replied. "So, you think you know the man in the video?"

"I do. His name is Marty. No, Monty. Sorry."

"And his last name?"

"Honestly, I don't recall. I didn't actually spend a lot of time with him."

"That's okay," Ramona said. "Do you have any idea where he lives or where we might find him?"

"I visited his house once," Sheila said.

Ramona couldn't help but notice the wave of goosebumps which suddenly populated her arms.

The girl continued, "It's not something I care to think about."

"Can you remember the address?"

"No, but I'm pretty sure I can find it."

"Where did you meet him?"

"Have you ever heard of a place called the Deep Six?"

Ramona tried not to make a face or do anything else which might offend the younger woman or otherwise reflect her distaste. "Yes," she said. "I've heard of it."

"They've got great chili," Sheila said.

"I'll take your word for it." Ramona smiled. "Would you mind showing me where this Monty character lives? I'm going to call my friend, the Sheriff, and see if he can join us."

"Sheriff *Odum?*" Sheila asked.

Ramona nodded.

"That's my boyfriend's uncle."

Ramona lit up. "*You're* the one who's dating Bubba!"

Sheila's grin confirmed it. "We haven't been together long. I've never met anyone quite like him. Will's a really great guy."

"*Will?*"

"Yeah. That whole 'Bubba' thing struck me as childish. He's a grown man with a perfectly good name, and I intend to use it."

The remark seemed altogether mature and reasonable. She liked the girl and the way she thought. "Ya know, I believe we're going to get along just fine." Then she called Odell. "I'm headed your way. I've got a lead on the guy in our video, and I'd like you to come with us to track him down."

"Don't you dare go anywhere near him without me," Odell warned. "Promise!"

Ramona's enthusiasm took on a chill of apprehension. "Okay, hon. I promise."

"Hon?" Sheila chuckled. "*You're* the one who's dating Will's uncle!"

~*~

The phone in Bubba's office rang several times before he could get to it. The county wanted him to answer the Center's phone with something approaching a professional tone, and Bubba did his best. "Thank you for calling the Charles County Convention Center. How can I help you?"

"My little group is looking for a place to meet," said the caller. "I thought it might be nice to use the Convention Center, assuming we can afford it."

"I'm sure we can help," Bubba said, trying to remember some of the hints Sheila had given him about salesmanship. Being positive and friendly were at the top of the list. "Did you have a date and time in mind?"

"It's rather last minute. I hope that won't be a problem."

"Probably not," said Bubba. "The schedule isn't crowded at the moment." He had no intention of telling her just how uncrowded it was. Hopefully, with Sheila's help, he would be able to improve on that. "Can I have your name, and the name of your club?"

"I'm Alexis Rae," the caller said. "And my group doesn't really have a name yet. We're still very new. In fact, I was hoping we'd come up with a name when we get together right there in the Convention Center. Is there an opening for this Saturday?"

"Wow, that is short notice. But I think you're in luck. Lemme look." Though he knew the Center hadn't been booked, he pretended to check the schedule just in case. The only thing he had going on was his monthly National Guard obligation. "Oddly enough, no one's booked any time slots on Saturday."

"Wonderful," she said. "Please hold the daytime slot for me. We'll meet in the late afternoon, but I'd like to drop by earlier and get everything set up."

"That shouldn't be a problem," Bubba said. "Just fill out the forms on our website, and let me know how you'll handle the fee."

"I hope it's not too terribly expensive," she said. "We're not a very big group."

Bubba smiled knowing Sheila would approve. "I tell you what, since this will be your first experience with the Center, I'm hoping we can provide everything you might need. Further, I'd like to offer our facility for all your future meetings. So, how 'bout we just do this first one on the house. As long as you clean up when you're done, we won't charge you a nickel."

"Oh, my. That's awfully generous."

"Just fill out the forms. That'll make the county folk happy, and I'll see to it you can get in to prepare for you event."

"You're just so nice," she said. "I can't thank you enough.

Chapter Twelve

"They say that women talk too much, but if you have ever worked in Congress, you know that the filibuster was invented by men." – Claire Booth Luce

Once again, Sheila found herself doing something she never thought she would ever do. Though she'd had several rides in cop cars, this was the first time she'd ever ridden shotgun.

If my old friends could see me now, she thought, then realized she didn't really have any old friends. Or any young ones, for that matter.

"Turn left up ahead," she said, and Sheriff Odum dutifully followed her instructions. Not too long ago, the very thought of sitting in a police vehicle would have made her nervous, if not anxious enough to look for a place to hide. This time, however, if felt... nice. It felt like she belonged.

"This street?" he asked.

"I'm pretty sure this is it," she said, peering intently at the houses they passed. Most looked far nicer than the one she'd fled after the massive error in judgment which landed her in Monty's bed. She struggled to repress shudders as memories of tequila and things that skittered in the dark ran through her mind. Ratting Monty out would go a long way toward settling the score with him.

"That's it!" she said, pointing at Monty's house. "He lives right there, in that nasty thing."

"You're sure?" Ramona asked from the back seat.

"Abso-blinking-lutely! If you ask me, the building ought to be bulldozed and burned for the sake of public health."

Will's uncle brought the squad car to a halt in Monty's driveway. The cracks in the pavement promised a challenging walk to the front door. "I can't help but wonder how you know this character."

"I... Uh... Know what? I'd rather not say. It's not something I'm proud of, and I'd just as soon not mention it to Will." She looked into the Sheriff's eyes. "Would that be too terrible?"

"Not if it happened before you met Bubba. I mean Will."

"It did."

"In that case," Ramona chimed in, "Worry not. You aren't required to divulge the details of every bad decision you've ever made to someone new in your life. Down the road... Well, who knows? That's up to you."

"She's right," said the Sheriff. "You'd do well to listen to her." He left the car before she could respond, then turned and looked back inside, his eyes moving swiftly between one woman and the other. "I've got the warrant. If this Monty character is here, I'll need to bring him in. If so, y'all will just have to scrunch up together in the front seat." He unlocked he rear doors so they could get out.

Sheila felt an immediate wave of relief knowing she wouldn't have to sit next to the creep.

"Wait here," the Sheriff said before he turned and walked toward the house.

Ramona stood just outside the car, watching her boyfriend approach the home of the miscreant. "You don't think Monty would try anything, do you?"

"I honestly can't say." Sheila crossed her fingers. "I certainly hope not. But, from what I've seen, he's mostly hot air. If a real man faced him, I'm sure he'd back down."

Ramona grimaced. "I hope you're right."

The two waited while the Sheriff went from the front door to the rear of the house. Eventually, he returned to the car. "He either wasn't home, or wasn't answering the doorbell."

"It figures. His car's gone," Sheila said.

The Sheriff ushered them both back into his car. "I can always come back later, now that I know where he lives."

~*~

Lacing up her skates for their last practice session, Willa Mae paused and exhaled in what she hoped would seem like a dramatic fashion.

Ramona responded with a characteristic rolling of her eyes. "Okay, what's the deal?"

"I'm still upset that nobody's caught the clown who's been poisoning our flowers."

"The infamous Monty?"

"Yeah." Willa Mae tightened the knots on her skates.

"He sounds like a game show host."

"We'll get him. He's on the run, but he can't get far," Ramona said. "Odell assured me of that."

"Not that it matters much. None of those who had their gardens ruined will stand a chance in the contest."

"We need to make an executive decision," Ramona said. "I agree it's not fair. I'm just not sure how we should handle it."

Willa Mae straightened up. "Well, now that you mention it, I might just have a solution. Interested?"

"You bet! I'm all ears."

~*~

Hildie repeated her new name over and over in hopes it would begin to sound natural to her. It didn't. But that didn't stop her. It gave her something to do as she sat in her rental car outside the Charles County Convention Center. There was only one other car in the lot, and she prayed it didn't belong to anyone she knew in her previous life.

She felt confident it didn't belong to the young man who took care of the place. She'd met him any number of times while setting up for her garden club meetings and prayed he wouldn't recognize her voice. He hadn't seemed to on the phone.

Taking a deep breath, she walked to the building and tried the front door. Locked, just as she feared. Another deep breath. She knocked and waited.

Footsteps. *If it's him, will he remember me?*

Fortunately, it wasn't him. Instead, a smiling young woman greeted her. "Mrs. Rae?" she asked.

"It's Miss," Hildie said, returning her smile. She'd never

seen the girl before.

"Come in, come in. Will told me you'd be dropping by. I'm Sheila. Is there anything I can help you with?"

"No, thank you. I'll be fine. If you'll just show me where to set up, I'll get started. It may take me quite a while."

"There's no hurry at all," Sheila said. "I've got some errands to run this afternoon, so you'll have the whole place to yourself."

Hildie followed her through the familiar foyer to the improbably named "Grand Ballroom."

"You're sure you don't need anything?" Sheila asked again. "We've got some soft drinks and snacks kicking around in the back."

Hildie patted her stomach. "Oh, I wish I could, but that stuff goes straight to the wrong places."

Sheila laughed and pointed to her hips with both hands. "Don't I know it!"

A quick look around the room revealed a number of large posters featuring athletic looking women on roller skates. Hildie pointed to one. "What's that all about?"

Sheila explained about the charity event and how it was being jointly sponsored by two garden clubs. "I think it's a great cause," she added. "And there's a big trophy under that sheet at the front of the room. It'll be awarded right after the skating event. It's a pretty big deal."

Oh, darlin', you have no idea just how big a deal it is.

"I hope the trophy won't get in your way, but it has to stay where it is until the day of the event. Then we'll have someone come in and move it." She leaned in and lowered her voice. "Will told me it's heavy as… well… Real heavy."

"It won't be in my way at all," Hildie assured her. "Now you go on about your business, and don't give me another thought. I can handle the set-up."

"Great. I'll drop by later this afternoon in case you change your mind." With that, Sheila walked casually through a back door and disappeared into the far reaches of the building.

Hildie puttered around the room, adjusting tables and chairs for her imaginary meeting, all the while waiting for Sheila to hop in her car and leave. The real work couldn't begin until she had the building all to herself.

When Sheila finally drove off, Hildie strode quickly to her car, opened the trunk, and removed a small but sturdy garden cart which she pushed into the Center and parked beside the covered trophy.

Removing the drape, she once again gazed upon the overdone prize she'd commissioned so many months earlier. It seemed like it had been years, but she knew better. Designing something so clearly ostentatious hadn't been easy and the craftsman who assembled it had offered any number of suggestions for making it less outrageous. She'd had to turn down every one of them in order to stay with her plan. The uglier the trophy, the less likely anyone would want to keep it in their home, thus making it easier for her to get to it. So far, that part of the plan had worked perfectly.

Using both hands, she gripped the glittery award by the top of the silver bucket and twisted it clockwise. Normally, that would have meant tightening it, but Hildie had demanded a reverse thread, so snoopy types would be less likely to figure out how to dismantle it.

It took a great deal of effort, but the flower laden top eventually moved, and Hildie eventually unscrewed the whole thing. She gently set it aside and dragged a chair closer so she'd have something to stand on as she unpacked everything she'd stored inside.

On her initial reach into the shiny garden pail, she encountered the first of many rolls of paper-wrapped coins. She hefted the first one, unable to keep from smiling at its surprising weight. She wondered if Cortez or any of the other old-world conquistadors had paused to enjoy the weight of pure gold. It seemed likely, although their mission had been to take the treasure to their queen. In Hildie's case, she *was* the queen.

Working steadily, she extracted roll after roll of gold coins. These she placed on a nearby table until she'd retrieved as much as she could conveniently transport in the little garden cart. She estimated it would require two trips, but that turned into three.

In addition to the cold coins, she also retrieved a small bag of diamonds Leonard had hidden away. Though easier to transport, it would require more effort to convert them into a spendable form. The gold coins would easily tide her over. She'd later call on the services of a helpful and creative banker in the Cayman Islands to liquidate the gems.

In the bag with the diamonds she recovered the thumb drive on which she'd stored copies of all her late husband's records. There had been too many illicit deals to bother counting. She'd leave that up to some district attorney somewhere. They'd make good use of it, and with any luck, they'd imprison the very criminals she knew were looking for her. She had an additional copy in her luggage if the worst happened, and she lost the trophy and its contents.

Once she'd secured the wagon and the valuables in her car, she carefully reconnected the trophy's top with its bottom and made sure it looked untouched. During the inspection she located something she knew she hadn't had installed, a tiny electronic gadget of some kind. The discovery brought her up short.

What if the room was under surveillance?

She quickly turned and scanned the room for cameras. Years earlier, before Leonard became a tool of the mob and found himself a girlfriend, they had taken a trip to Las Vegas. He pointed out the various forms of cameras employed by the casinos to keep an eye on the players. She hadn't given it much thought at the time, but now the memory came in handy.

Once she'd satisfied herself that she wasn't being recorded or observed, she pulled out a large manilla envelope on which she'd written Ramona Dorn's name. She put the thumb drive and an explanatory note inside and had almost sealed it when a new thought struck her.

Ramona had taken quite a risk just talking to her, and as far as Hildie could tell, she had kept silent about her garden club predecessor's return from the dead. In addition, she'd done amazing things with the organization, much more than Hildie ever did. The roller derby charity event proved that. So, in addition to the thumb drive, Hildie added one of the rolls of gold coins. She updated the note to indicate the gift should go toward the charity. She had no idea what a special needs playground would cost, but felt confident her contribution would be appreciated.

Leaving a note for someone in a sealed envelope was one thing, but leaving one worth thousands of dollars laying around was quite another. Hildie suffered a moment of indecision. She had no intention of trying to mail it. Too many of the post office staff had seen her over the years and might recognize her. Besides, on such short notice she lacked the necessary packing materials to do it right. In the end she simply sealed the coins, thumb drive, and note in the envelope and secured it among the gilded flowers atop the trophy. Then she replaced the drape. With any luck, Ramona would get it.

Finished, Hildie carefully wiped down everything in the room she'd touched. Changing her fingerprints hadn't been an option. From that moment on, only Alexis Rae could go forward. Hildegard Henderson was no more.

~*~

Odell's phone call came at an opportune moment. Ramona just taken a break from going over last-minute details for the derby. She'd received two frantic calls from senior members of both clubs expressing concern about the team colors to be used in their cheering gear. Ramona took pains to assure them that anything they found that was even remotely close would be perfectly fine.

"Hey, sweetie. Got any news for me about the garden ghoul?"

"Garden ghoul?" Odell asked.

"That's how the paper described him. Willa Mae has some amazing connections. She even got them to put the article on the front page."

"Maybe you could get her to have them say something nice about the department."

"I can certainly ask. So, news?" Ramona felt like a puppy begging for a treat.

"Actually," he said, his voice slow and cautious, "I do have some news."

"Tell me; tell me!"

"I suspect you may not like it."

"Let me be the judge of that, okay? Now, spill."

"One of my deputies stopped our suspect for a traffic violation and noticed he had an outstanding warrant. The idiot tried to bribe my guy. And, are you ready for this? He had less than twenty bucks on him."

Ramona laughed. "What's the going rate for bribes these days?"

"There ain't one in this county," he said, slightly wounded.

"I'm kidding."

"I know."

"So, you've got him locked up? I'd love to see him. Maybe take his picture so the whole club can see him." She actually liked that idea.

"Sorry, no can do. Rules."

"Rules? Seriously? What moron put those into effect?"

Odell chuckled. "The same morons who added the Bill of Rights to the Constitution."

"Oh." *Geez…*

"Article 8. Something about cruel and unusual punishment."

Ramona groaned. "Gotcha. I know that one. I just didn't think taking his picture—"

"And plastering it all over town?"

"Well, not *all* over."

"It doesn't matter," Odell said. "Somebody already bailed him out."

Ramona gasped. "So fast?"

"Unfortunately, yes. See, we don't have a lot of space to house misdemeanor types, so the county does what it can to move them out quickly."

"Well, just... darn. Do you know who paid his bail?"

"No, but his kind usually work it out with one of the bail bondsmen in town." He whistled. "Talk about a racket."

"Is there any way you could find out?"

"I guess, if it means that much to you."

"I'll make your favorite dessert." Ramona used her best breathy voice.

"Babe, *you* are my favorite dessert."

She giggled, and then felt stupid. *How does he do that?* "Okay then, how's this? If you can tell me who bailed Monty out, I'll find a way to add something special to your favorite dessert."

"I'm tempted," he said. "Would it involve whipped cream?"

"It could." She giggled again.

"Okay then, lemme put you on hold for a sec."

A second? Is that all the longer it took? She'd been saving the nightie she bought to celebrate their second monthiversary. Then she smiled. *If I want to wear something new and different, this'll give me the excuse to find another.*

Odell came back on the line a moment later. "Okay," he said. "I got it."

"Was it a bail bondsman?"

"Nope. Private citizen."

"Do I know them?"

Odell laughed. "How on Earth would I know that?"

"Just give me the dadgum name, okay?" She felt ready to burst.

"The name on the file is a Mrs. Constance DuBois. I'm not sure of the pronunciation."

"Spell it, please."

He did.

"Connie," Ramona breathed. "That dirty, underhanded bit—"

"Now, now," Odell said. "We don't know if she had anything to do with ol' Monty's shenanigans."

"You may not," Ramona grumbled. "But I do."

~*~

Sheila took her time since Will wouldn't be done with his Guard duty until dinnertime. She wanted to fix something nice for him, though she wasn't much of a cook. That just meant she'd have to follow the instructions carefully. She'd bought a small roast, mostly because the cooking requirements were spelled out clearly on the label. Besides Will wasn't fussy; it wasn't in his nature. He loved being loved. For that matter, so did she.

Making something special for dinner wasn't the only thing she had on her mind. She'd found a variety of pregnancy test kits to choose from, and selected one almost at random. Though eager to know for sure, a notice on the box advised that she wait until she first woke up to take the test. Supposedly, that would help ensure accuracy.

She hadn't said anything yet to Will. He had plenty on his mind with the fire department training and his National Guard stuff. There would be a good time soon enough. And she decided, since she didn't have to say anything about it that evening, she left the test kit in her purse.

With a plastic bag of groceries in each hand, Sheila made her way toward the kitchen and living quarters at the rear of the Center. This required her to walk through the main hall where she expected to see some preparations for the evening's event, supposedly a small gathering.

Instead of decorations or carefully arranged tables and chairs, the room didn't appear very different from the way it had when she left earlier in the day. Some things had been moved around a bit, but the room certainly wasn't ready for anything special.

She noticed the drape had been rearranged on the garden club trophy at the front of the room. A table and chair had been shoved next to it.

Sheila approached it slowly, a habit of caution evolved from a lifetime of sneakiness. She set her groceries on the table and carefully removed the drape from the shiny, bauble-encrusted trophy. Nearly at eye level, and lightly woven between the flower stems, sat a large manilla envelope. Ramona Dorn's name had been scrawled across the front of it in large letters.

What the heck was this about?

A more pressing question popped into her head when she removed the envelope and realized how heavy it was. The stiff paper yielded little information, and she guessed it held a short length of lead pipe.

"Well, why not?" she asked herself out loud. "What's so strange about a woman hiding a chunk of lead pipe in a business envelope for another woman?"

Sure.

She inspected the envelope more closely in hopes of opening it without damaging the seal. But that option quickly evaporated. If she wanted to investigate further, she'd have to rip open the glued-down flap.

Or steam it open! She'd done it before, but with mixed results. Cheap white envelopes opened fairly easily when exposed to steam, although the paper sometimes rippled. She'd never experimented with a manilla one.

There was plenty of time. Will wouldn't be home for a couple hours at the earliest, and it didn't appear Miss Ra would be coming back.

Sheila slipped Ramona Dorn's mysterious missive into a grocery bag and carried everything into the kitchen. After putting away the groceries, she focused her considerable attention on the light brown envelope.

There was no teapot in the kitchen, so she filled a small aluminum pan with water and set it on the stove to boil. Once the steam roiled above the bubbling water, she carried the weighty envelope toward it.

And stopped.

What the hell am I doing?

She took a step back and glanced at Ramona Dorn's name. The woman had been nice to her. But she was dating Will's uncle, *a lawman*, for God's sake! What if she couldn't reseal the envelope? What if—

"It's not like there's any postage on it," she muttered. "So, technically, it's not really mail. And there's nothing written on here to indicate it's personal or confidential. None of that."

Sometimes, she told herself, a mystery just cried out to be solved, and this one certainly qualified. If she messed up the envelope, she'd just have to get another one and write Ramona's name on it. She could probably come close to duplicating the existing penmanship. Surely Will would understand and back her up.

Surely.

Heck with it. I'm in.

She held the sealed end of the envelope over the boiling water, taking care to avoid having steam collect on the paper and condense into droplets. Several quick, successive applications did the trick.

Sheila carefully pried open the glued flap and let the contents of the envelope slide out onto a kitchen counter. She made sure the flap wouldn't reseal while she investigated what she'd found.

The thumb drive didn't interest her much. She wasn't very well schooled in the use of computers. If not for the ancient PC the county had installed in the Convention Center, neither she nor Will would have had access to one.

The handwritten note was short and to the point. It thanked Ramona and suggested she give the thumb drive to the police. That gave Sheila even more reason not to look into it.

A hastily added note at the end, however, galvanized her attention. The coins, it said, were to be considered a donation for the playground project.

Sheila recalled hearing about the garden club's plans to provide slides and swing sets for crippled kids, but it hadn't interested her. The mention of coins, however, was an entirely different matter.

She hefted the roll of coins, trying to guess their denomination. Fifty-cent pieces? They seemed far too heavy for that. And why make such a big deal about donating a few dollars in coins?

Time to dig deeper, she thought as she carefully unwrapped the tight roll and spread the contents on the counter: gold coins. Twenty of them. One shiny troy ounce each.

Sheila put her hand to her cheek and stared down at the gleaming treasure as an image of an open pirate's chest zipped through her brain. She didn't know exactly what gold sold for, but she felt certain she'd heard someone on the news saying it had risen well above $1,500 an ounce. A quick mental calculation suggested the coins spread out in front of her were worth $30,000. At the very least.

She had to sit down.

Thirty grand was far more than anything she'd ever scored in her entire, score-filled life.

Thirty freaking grand!

~*~

Ramona was shocked when Constance DuBois answered her phone call, and she told her so.

Connie responded in a thoroughly bored fashion. "I mustn't take much."

"Why did you bail him out?" asked Ramona.

"What are you talking about?"

"Monty What's-his-name. You bailed him out of jail. I want to know why."

"Oh, that." Connie exhaled in long-suffering fashion. "I don't believe that's any of your business."

"*Au contraire*," Ramona said, feeling free to vent. "It'

entirely my business. He's the one who's been killing off flowers in competitor's gardens."

"So they say."

"So says the video we have of him doing it."

There was a distinct pause before Connie spoke. "I don't believe you."

"How did you think we identified him?"

"Doesn't matter," Connie said. "My grandson would never do anything like that."

"Monty is your *grandson?*" Ramona snorted. "That explains a lot."

"What's that supposed to mean?"

"It strikes me as ironic that of the dozen or so people vying for the Henderson prize, yours was one of the few gardens that went unscathed by the vandal. And now we learn you're related to him. Imagine that."

"Imagine whatever you like," Connie said, her voice flat. "We'll see how you like it when people find out you're trying to slander my grandson and accuse me of cheating."

Connie hung up before Ramona could answer, but she responded anyway. "It's not slander if it's true. And if you're so darned innocent, sue me!"

Chapter Thirteen

"Any time women come together with a collective intention, it's a powerful thing. Whether it's sitting down making a quilt, in a kitchen preparing a meal, in a club reading the same book, around a table playing cards, or planning a birthday party, when women come together with a collective intention, magic happens."
– Phylicia Rashad

Willa Mae looked at herself in the full-length mirror which dominated the walk-in closet of the master bedroom. She had never been keen on wearing anything that put her legs on display as she'd always thought they were a bit too fleshy.

She wasn't sure if it was merely her imagination, but as she gazed at her reflection, it seemed her legs looked slightly more athletic. Of course, it might have simply been the fancy leggings or the curve-hugging short-shorts she wore, both of which she would never have considered before she got roped into the derby stunt. Now, however, she thought she looked pretty darned good for a gal her age. And she didn't mind in the least the additional attention she'd been getting from her husband, Robert. He'd even insisted that she pose for photos in her derby gear.

The purple jersey she wore looked pretty darned good, too. Twisting from the waist, she could just make out her derby name emblazoned on the back, "Killa Willa." She and Ramona had laughed about the names they'd chosen, each attempting to out-do the other. Their friendship surprised them both. It didn't mean they wouldn't compete as hard as they could, but it was a comfort to know they'd still be friends when it was over.

Her two boys, both in high school, had rolled their eyes and given her no end of grief when the idea first came up. But more recently they'd been quite supportive, and they asked if they could bring their friends along to watch the match. Willa Mae encouraged them to recruit all their friends, and all their families, too. It was, after all, a charity event.

She smiled at herself. This was going to be fun.

~*~

"I don't suppose there's any way you could arrest Connie DuBois, is there?"

Odell put his arm around Ramona's shoulders and hugged her. "I'm afraid not, darlin'. Suspicion is one thing; facts are something else. If we arrested everyone somebody *assumed* had broken the law, our jails would stretch from one side of the county to the other."

"I have no doubt she put her sleazy grandson up to it."

"That may be, but it's going to be tough to prove."

Ramona smiled wickedly. "Unless he admitted it. Couldn't you smack him around a little bit to loosen his tongue?"

Odell laughed. "You've been watching way too many late-night movies. Law enforcement these days should be

community focused, nuanced I'm told, gentle for the mos
part. We only break legs when some does something reall
outrageous."

"Like double-parking."

"Yeah. Like that."

Ramona rested her head on his shoulder. "You're a
nut. I guess that's why I love you."

"That's high praise indeed, coming from 'Ram-moan
ah.'"

"And don't you forget it!"

"Y'know," he said, his voice dropping into a seriou
register, "there's likely a lot more to all this Leonar
Henderson business than we know about. There's a piece o
the puzzle we just don't have."

"I thought the GBI was looking into it," Ramona said
"That's not your job, is it?"

"No, it's not," he said. "But that doesn't mean I don'
have to worry about it. That's why I intend to have a coupl
extra guys on hand at the derby."

"Seriously?" Ramona laughed. "Do you honestly thin
some drug cartel goons care about a garden club charit
event?"

"Nah." He patted her arm. "I guess you're right. I'm jus
being overly protective."

"That part's okay," she said, snuggling closer. "Fee
free to protect me all you want."

~*~

Bubba arrived home a little later than usual, whic
didn't sit well with him. He'd been looking forward t

spending the evening with Sheila. If pressed on the point, he would have admitted being distracted by thoughts of her for most of the day.

"Babe?" he called. "I'm home."

She hurried through the main room to greet him by the foyer with a huge hug and a kiss. "Oh, man, am I ever glad to see you!"

"What's up?" he asked after a hug that had his fantasies firing on all cylinders.

"I've just missed you," she said, kissing him again.

He thought that sounded a tiny bit suspicious. "Okay, what's *really* up?"

"Well," she said, letting the word play out dramatically. "Do you remember the lady you talked to about having an event this evening? You told me to be on the lookout for her and let her in so she could set the place up."

"Sure." He looked at the dimly lit hall. "I'm surprised they haven't started yet."

"They should have started about an hour ago."

"Oh?" He took a few steps into the room and looked around. "It doesn't look to me like she did anything."

Sheila nodded. "That was my reaction, too. But it turns out she actually *did* do something."

He turned a puzzled gaze her way.

"Follow me," she said. Taking his hand, she led him through the main hall and into the kitchen where she came to a halt and pointed at the room's central counter. "Check that out."

Bubba moved in and bent down for a closer look. He'd

never seen real, live gold coins before and suspected the were phony. "These are fake, right?"

"Not as far as I can tell," she said. "Pick one up. I certainly feels real to me. I used the computer to look them up online. "They're one-ounce, American Gold Eagles. Have you any idea what they're worth?"

Bubba shook his head, not quite able to form coherent thoughts.

"Around sixteen hundred bucks a pop."

He looked at her in wonder.

"That's thirty-two thousand dollars in all," she said her voice barely above a whisper.

"Holy cow." It was all he could muster. "Where'd you get them?"

She showed him the envelope with Ramona Dorn' name on it. "They were in this, along with a note saying she should add them to the proceeds from the garden club charity."

Bubba eased himself away from the counter and slowly focused on Sheila. "They belong to someone else."

She nodded. "That woman you talked to on the phone Alexis Rae, she left them behind. In that envelope. It's like she knew I'd find it and open it. Who wouldn't?"

"I don't know about anyone else, but you *did* open it Even though it was addressed to someone else."

"Well, yeah. I mean it was just sitting there, and—"

"Aw, geez, Sheila. What if she finds out?"

She looked him right in the eye and laughed. "What makes you think she'd find out? She's gone, babe. Her whole meeting thing was bogus, a sham. I have no idea what she's got cooked up, but conducting some sort of club event, here, tonight, is about as likely as the Easter Bunny showing up with cocktails for us. It ain't gonna happen."

"This is crazy," he said. "I— I don't understand."

Sheila stepped closer and wrapped her arms around him. "This is a sign, sweetheart. I don't know if it's coming from God or the patron saint of lost souls, but it's a sign. For us. It's a chance to have a running start at life. Geez, Will. Thirty-two thousand dollars just fell into our lap!"

Bubba's head spun. He'd seen the commercials that featured people who won the Publisher's Sweepstakes. He'd seen the celebrations of the people who owned the horses that won the Kentucky Derby. He'd seen Super Bowl winners and World Series winners celebrate, with champagne sprays and wild cheers, but he'd never imagined himself in their place.

"Wow," he said.

"Wow?" Sheila looked incredulous. "That's it? Wow?"

He swallowed, hard. "You know I love you, right?"

"Yes! Of course."

"For the first time in my life, I feel like things are starting to come together for me. I mean, before I found you, I had no one, nothing. I had a stupid job and dumb dreams, but I didn't have anything that truly meant anything. Do you understand what I'm saying?"

She squinted at him. "I think so, yeah."

"And then, from out of the clear blue, you're in my life. And my dumb dreams suddenly don't seem so stupid."

"They aren't stupid," she said. "They never were!"

"Let me finish." He wiped at his eyes. "Remember when we talked about stealing the gemstones from the trophy?"

"Yeah."

"We decided that was a bad idea, didn't we?"

She bobbed her head.

He swallowed again, even harder than before. "I don't want to steal anything from anybody, especially not some poor little kids who're stuck in wheelchairs."

"Aw, geez, Will—"

"Let me finish, okay?" He took a deep breath. "I understand thirty-two thousand dollars is a lot of money. More than I've ever seen at one time in my whole life. And if you're bound and determined to grab it and run, I'll understand. I won't say a word to anybody."

"Will—"

"Hang on. If you think that'll make you happy, then I'm fine with it. Take the coins and go. Have a wonderful life. Do whatever you want. I won't tell a soul."

"*Will!*"

"What?"

"I love you," she said. "I'd much rather have you than thirty-two thousand dollars. I'd rather have you than thirty-two *million* dollars."

"Seriously?"

She laughed. "Okay. Thirty-two million might require a whole different mindset."

He gathered her in his arms and hugged her tight. "We don't need to steal anything. We've got each other."

"Have you any idea how corny that sounds?"

"Yes. No. I dunno. I don't care," he said. "We've got a chance at a decent life. Why throw it away for money?"

"'Cause money makes the world go 'round?"

He smiled. "I wouldn't trade you for anything. No way."

She kissed him full on the mouth, and he responded with ferocity.

"Hang on there, tiger," she said.

"Why? What? What'd I do?"

"Nothing." She shifted so she could see his face. "I just wanted to say how proud I am of you. I'm not going anywhere."

"And the money?"

"I'm going to put the coins back in the envelope, seal it up, and whenever you're ready, we'll take it to Mrs. Dorn."

Bubba felt a tear and quickly wiped it away. "I love you."

Sheila hugged him again. "I love you, too, babe. I really, really do."

~*~

Things had gone reasonably well, Hildie thought, as she looked over the valuables she'd retrieved. The only remaining roadblock was the liquidation of the coins arrayed in front of her. That would require the services of a number of firms. She had no desire to raise any flags with regulators by trying to move it all through just one or two companies. She needed a bunch.

That meant she would have to stay in the area for a while longer. Day trips to larger towns wouldn't be so bad, and for that purpose, St. Charlotte seemed strategically located. She might even stick around and watch the roller derby, something she hadn't thought about since her childhood. That might be fun.

But having some fun meant little compared to the very real possibility that Leonard's gangster pals might figure out what happened to the cash he'd stolen from them. According to what she read in the paper, they'd already searched every place with which Leonard was connected. At some point they'd have to wonder about the lavish trophy she'd commissioned.

Now that her future was all but secured, she could afford to worry about the safety of others, most notably the good people in the St. Charlotte Garden Club.

~*~

Ramona had gotten a call from Odell's nephew who wanted to know if she planned to be home for a while as he and his girlfriend wanted to drop by for a visit.

"We won't stay long, I promise," he'd said.

She assured him she'd be home. "What's this about?"

"It's a surprise," he said. "A good one."

"Can you give me a hint?"

"Okay. Do you know someone named Alexis Rae?"

She couldn't recall ever meeting anyone by that name. "Nope. It's not familiar."

He remained silent for a moment longer than necessary, then continued. "Well, whatever. Maybe you'll remember her when you see what we have."

Their brief conversation played on her mind as she waited. She did the breakfast dishes, what few there were, and reviewed a pile of mail she'd let accumulate. She found nothing exciting there and turned on the TV. The screen quickly filled with the usual selection of game shows, movies that should have been retired long ago, and political commentary, none of which interested her.

Alexis Rae?

At long last she heard a car in the driveway and walked to the door to greet her guests. She watched as Bubba and Sheila walked toward her hand-in-hand. Sheila carried a large manilla envelope.

"Want some coffee?" Ramona asked after ushering them inside.

"Like I said on the phone, we won't stay long." Bubba turned to Sheila and gave his head a tiny nod.

"This is yours," the younger woman said. "Someone by the name of Alexis Rae left it for you."

"Yikes," Ramona said, hefting the package. "I wonder what's in it?"

"They're coins," Sheila said. "Very special coins."

"We opened it," Bubba said. "We shouldn't have, and I apologize for that."

"It was just me, actually," confessed Sheila. "Curiosity got the best of me."

Ramona glanced at the sealed envelope and frowned. "It doesn't appear to have been opened."

Sheila's mouth twisted. "That's 'cause I resealed it. I was very careful. This is really embarrassing. I'm sorry. I shouldn't have done it." She put her hand on Ramona's arm. "But you really need to see what's in it. It's important."

Ramona wasted no time tearing open the envelope and dumping out the contents: a note, a thumb drive, and what appeared to be a roll of coins. She picked up the note first and quickly read through it. The handwriting was quite familiar, but the message made everything clear. The message wasn't signed, but she knew who wrote it.

"How is it you know this Alexis person?" Ramona asked.

"She called, and I asked her to sign into the Convention Center website," Bubba said. He explained about her request to set the place up for a meeting which never happened. "She came in and left that envelope, then disappeared. The phone number she left turned out to be a car wash somewhere near Valdosta. They'd never heard of her."

"I'm not surprised." Ramona stared at the thumb drive, then looked straight at them. "I need you to erase any record of her. Website, notepads, everything."

"Why?"

"It's important that no one knows she exists." She paused, not sure how to express the gravity of her request. "Please, just trust me."

"Will you promise to discuss this with Uncle Odell?"

"Absolutely."

"Okay then," he said, "no problem."

"Now, quick, unwrap the coins," Sheila said, sounding every bit like an over-excited schoolgirl. "You're gonna flip."

Ramona unfolded the paper wrapper and let the coins spill out on her kitchen counter. "Oh. My. God!"

Sheila giggled. "Is that cool, or what?" She picked up a coin and held it between her thumb and forefinger for closer inspection. "How much money do you need to raise in order to build the playground?"

"We've had several estimates. They're not cheap. We'll build as much as we can afford."

Bubba and Sheila smiled at each other, then at Ramona. "With what you'll get for those coins, you're gonna be able to build something really special," Bubba said.

Ramona hugged them both and thanked them for coming by. "You've made my day. And while I can't say I'm happy that you opened the envelope, I'm impressed by your honesty."

She watched them leave, wrapped up in each other like teenage lovers. But as they drove off, her thoughts shifted to the thumb drive. That was something she needed to turn over to Odell, and the sooner, the better.

As agreed, Willa Mae met the derby teams as they drifted in from Savannah and Atlanta and checked into one of St. Charlotte's two surviving motels. Traveler's Rest, the larger of the two, sat on two wooded acres at the edge of town and had agreed to serve as the official host for the exhibition match. Willa Mae herself had talked them into offering a discount provided all the visitors stayed there.

The motel featured a swimming pool, and several of the skaters made themselves comfortable in it while waiting for their teammates and volunteer support staff to arrive. Willa Mae would escort them all to the armory once everyone had checked in.

Eventually, full complements from both cities reached St. Charlotte. They formed a caravan and followed Willa Mae as she drove to the National Guard post. Once there, they were met by a frowning Col. Lovejoy who insisted on observing any and all preparations to insure nothing in the armory was damaged. That slowed the preparations as he seemed to have questions about everything from the placement of the armory's built-in bleachers to the use of painter's tape on the floor to outline the derby track.

Willa Mae merely stood back and watched as the skaters and their entourage went to work. No strangers to this sort of set-up, the process went much faster than she would have thought possible, despite Col. Lovejoy's interference.

When they finished, everyone piled back into their vehicles and returned to the Traveler's Rest where they would wrap up their preparations for the evening match. Ramona showed up about that time having made a last appeal on the local radio station for folks to come out and support the event.

Jocelyn Bishop, Ramona's contact with the Atlanta team offered to help them both with their make-up.

"I don't want it to look too extreme," Ramona said.

Jocelyn appeared puzzled. "Why not? It's part of what makes the derby so much fun. Everyone tends to go a little over the top. C'mon, Ram-*moan-ah*."

"I can't wait to look like a wild woman," Willa Mae said. "I'd love to scare the livin' daylights outta my two boys.'

Jocelyn chuckled. "I'll do my best. You'll have to rely on attitude for the rest."

Seeing all the other skaters taking time to make themselves look "exotic" helped. Willa Mae found her pulse consistently more rapid than usual.

It won't be long now. Dear God, please don't let me look stupid!

~*~

Ramona had told Odell about Annabelle and her band of aging cheerleaders. He'd thought their antics would only result in embarrassment. Instead, the two squads of colorfully dressed older women performed admirably. The crowd, which had waited outside the building, filed in after paying admission and formed up on either side of the wide-open assembly area. St. Charlotte fans gathered at the north end of the building while fans of the county club assembled to the south.

Alternating chants of "City Club" and "County Club" rattled the metal rafters, thanks to the cheer squads. Food and beverage carts, which one of the senior club members somehow got permission to operate, provided a decent selection of beer, wine, and snacks for the surprisingly large audience. The beverages certainly added to both the volume and the spirit of the cheers.

Col. Lovejoy approached Odell as the chants and cheers continued. "I never thought so many people would turn out for this... whatever it is."

"We call it fun," Odell said. "It's different, interesting. And it's for a good cause."

"That's what I'm told." Lovejoy crossed his arms. "I'm glad you're in uniform, and I hope you have additional staff on hand in case this thing goes sideways."

"We've got an ambulance and EMTs standing by, and my deputies can and will respond quickly if needed."

At that point, an announcer from the local radio station took to the center of the track, microphone in hand. "Ladies and gentlemen, old and young, your attention please!"

The crowd quickly settled down.

"Welcome to the first ever St. Charlotte/Charles

County Roller Derby Extravaganza! It is my great honor to introduce you to the two fabulous teams who will compete this evening, along with their honorary captains."

As he spoke, the teams formed up on opposite sides of the rink. Ramona looked stunning in her fishnet tights and neon green jersey. Her counterpart from the county club looked equally sexy, and both women waved excitedly.

"Let's hear it for the team captains: 'Killa Willa' Sundee for the Charles County Cuties, and 'Ram-moan-ah' Dorn for the St. Charlotte Charlatans!"

It warmed Odell's heart to see such an outpouring of support, especially for the cheerleaders whom some dimwit on the editorial staff at *The Chatter* had the nerve to describe as "superannuated." He'd had to look the word up only to discover it meant someone older than usual. Most cheerleaders, according to the self-proclaimed humorist, stopped cheerleading prior to their 70th birthday, which is when many of these fine ladies began. Obviously, the writer knew nothing about gardening folk. The response to the op-ed had been overwhelmingly negative.

The announcer continued and introduced the team from Atlanta and Savannah who were donating their time and energy for the cause. He directed everyone's attention to a large display at one end of the hall which offered some ideas about how the special needs playground might work. Thanks to the combined efforts of both clubs, three different manufacturers had arranged to have samples of their wares delivered and displayed on-site.

Almost as an afterthought, he mentioned the flamboyant trophy which would be awarded at halftime to the winner of the inaugural Hildegard Henderson Horticultural contest. The trophy looked a bit forlorn on its pedestal, although the heavy gold rope on mounting stand borrowed from the local theater gave it a bit of glitz and glamor. Odell wondered why they'd set it up so close to the exit and assumed it was an attempt to make sure everyone saw it.

At last the announcer called everyone's attention to the evening's first round of competition. He rattled off the names of the first five skaters from each team. Willa Mae and Ramona would enter the fray in the second jam.

Odell uttered a short, silent prayer for Ramona's safety. The derby was, after all, his idea, and if she got hurt, he'd never hear the end of it.

Sheila stood beside Will at the entrance to the armory as people jostled into seats and balanced premium beverages, over-sized pretzels, and clueless offspring. An air of curious expectation hung thick above the crowded room.

"You come here one weekend every month," Sheila said. "What do you do?"

"Well," Will said, "we've got a new guy in charge, so things may change. But mostly what I've done is exercise the vehicles."

She looked at him as if he'd sprouted tentacles, and he got the hint.

"Basically, that means I drive some of our heavy gear around, make sure it's working properly in case we have to take it somewhere. There's no point in having an armored personnel carrier if it doesn't work."

"That makes sense," she said, then pressed closer and whispered in his hear. "Can you show me one?"

"Now? The derby's about to start."

"I'll make it worth your while," she said, her voice low and throaty. When she gently caressed his neck, he caved.

"C'mon. There's an MRAP right outside the front."

She had no idea what an em-wrap might be, but it didn't matter. Her primary goal was to get him out of the building where she could talk to him in private.

He escorted her to a huge armored vehicle and opened the driver side door. "This big ol' hunk of steel is called a 'mine-resistant, ambush protected vehicle.' MRAP for short. Climb in!"

"Won't we get in trouble?"

"Nah. Everybody else is inside watching the skaters." He gave her a boost up then followed her in. Once inside he pointed out the particulars, none of which interested her. They soon settled into the front seats.

"There's something I've been meaning to tell you," she began.

"Ya mean about how you're going to reward me for sneakin' you in here?"

She giggled. "Well, yes and no. But first things first."

He gave her his undivided attention.

"See, the thing is...." She paused, not completely happy with how she'd planned to proceed.

"What is it?"

She forced herself to smile. "How would you feel if I told you we were going to have a baby?"

Will's jaw dropped, and it took him a moment or two to gather his wits enough to respond. "You're— I mean, *we're* pregnant?"

"Yup."

"You're sure? I mean, really, *really* sure?"

"As sure as anyone can be. I haven't been to a doctor yet, but I used a pregnancy test, and they're supposed to be reliable."

"Oh, my gosh!" he exclaimed, grinning as broadly as humanly possible. "I'm gonna be a *dad?* Seriously?"

She basked in a flood of relief. "Assuming everything goes well. Yes, you're gonna be a daddy."

They embraced as best they could inside a vehicle designed for anything but that.

"Can you shove your seat back some?" she asked.

"Sure!" He reached under the seat for the lever which allowed the adjustment. The seat lurched backwards.

Sheila climbed up into his lap and turned to face him, her arms circling his head and shoulders. "Now, you remember that reward I promised you?"

Chapter Fourteen

"I haven't trusted polls since I read that 62% of women had affairs during their lunch hour. I've never met a woman in my life who would give up lunch for sex."
– Erma Bombeck

Though she now called herself Alexis, and had several official looking documents with which to prove it was true, she still thought of herself as Hildie Henderson. She still loved gardening, and she still treasured her friends. But she feared for their safety as a result of her own need to survive. All of that she blamed on Leonard, for whom she shed no tears.

Those she most worried about were the people inside the National Guard armory that evening. It would be her last night in St. Charlotte, a town she'd lived in most of her life, a town she loved.

She felt the pull of the crowd. There were many people inside whom she knew, people she longed to talk to and apologize to for her deception. But that would undo everything and likely put them in even greater danger.

Assuming Leonard's killers believed they could recoup their losses by stealing the trophy, they would quickly realize it was merely a gaudy reminder of a woman who loved flowers. Its value, at best, amounted to a trifling percentage of what had been taken from them. They might continue to look for her, but they'd be done with St. Charlotte. That was her greatest hope.

Unfortunately, the only way they could reach that conclusion was by stealing the trophy, and this event would provide a wonderful opportunity. Though not exactly a secret, the trophy's location hadn't been widely discussed, but since it would be awarded that evening, the paper had played it up, both for its gems and precious metals, and its location.

Hildie was determined to wait outside the venue and keep an eye out for the gangsters she thought might be coming. She had a pair of binoculars, and her cell phone sat close at hand, fully charged and ready. If they showed up, she felt sure she would recognize them, and she'd happily sound the alarm.

Though she had no way of knowing how things were proceeding inside, she could tell by the volume of crowd noise the event was in full swing. That didn't make the seat in her rental car any more comfortable. She had arrived early in the afternoon to make sure she observed everyone who came and went. By the time the fans showed up, her back and legs were stiff even though she'd gotten out of the car from time to time and moved around. Still, she waited.

Her patience was rewarded an hour or so after the scheduled start time. Two men pulled through the gate and into the parking lot. They turned their vehicle around to face the exit before double-parking it near the building entrance. Hildie didn't call 911 until she saw them exit their car carrying guns and a short length of heavy chain.

"9-1-1," the operator said. "What is your emergency?"

Garden Clubbed!

"I want to report a robbery in progress," Hildie said.

~*~

Ramona struggled to catch her breath after her third jam. She had no idea the real thing would be so tough. The practice session they'd endured with the teams from Atlanta and Savannah hadn't been nearly as challenging. She took some comfort knowing Willa Mae wheezed every bit as hard as she did.

In her last jam, she'd broken through Savannah's blockers twice and circled the field, racking up quite a few points. Willa Mae had yet to accomplish that feat, though not for lack of effort. Both of them had gone down more than once in a tangle of arms and legs, complements of solid hip thrusts from women who knew exactly what they were doing and who they were up against—pros versus amateurs.

The concrete floor was unyielding. Their pads and helmets saved them from the worst of it, but Ramona knew they'd both have some serious bruises come morning. Willa had looked surprisingly tough on the track with her scowl and downcast eyebrows. Now that they were on the sidelines resting, they both relaxed their game faces, and Willa actually looked a bit bewildered. She returned Ramona's smile from the opposite side of the track and mouthed the words, "This is hard!" Then she made a goofy face that cracked Ramona up.

Her laughter ended abruptly when she heard a shout and looked toward the entrance of the armory where Odel had stationed himself by the trophy. She didn't see him at first because she focused on two gun-carrying thugs. Odel lay at their feet, and he wasn't moving.

Ramona's heart went into overdrive as she watched one of the gunmen grab the trophy while the other manhandled Annabelle Knox who slapped ineffectually at him with her pompoms. Other voices chimed in as the men backed toward the door waving their weapons at the crowd.

In mere moments they'd left the building and shut the doors behind them. Just as quickly, a number of derby watchers left their seats and went hurtling toward the exit. But despite their combined efforts to open them, the doors yielded no more than an inch.

"They're getting away!" someone screamed.

"I don't care about that," yelled another. "They've got my mama!"

~*~

Pressed against the back of the driver's seat in the MRAP with Sheila in his lap, Bubba's mind surrendered to a sensory flood of romance. Neither could get enough of the other. His only regret centered on the limited amount of space between himself and the steering wheel, though it didn't seem to bother Sheila. She remained focused on him.

Fearing that someone in the parking lot might catch sight of them, Bubba cast a quick glance at the side mirror, praying he'd see nothing but empty cars. Instead, he saw two armed men, one of whom bore the garden club trophy under his arm while the other forced a woman old enough to be his grandmother to walk in front of him.

The fact that the elderly woman was clad in a brightly colored, plaid mini-skirt registered for just a split second. What had him completely floored was the ability of a man to carry the profoundly heavy trophy in one arm. Even though the guy stood taller than most people, he didn't look anything like a body builder. He was just a big, mean bully. And he was stealing the trophy!

"Hang on," he whispered into Sheila's ear.

"Oh, baby," she said as Bubba cranked up the MRAP's massive engine. The barely muffled growl got her attention. "*Will?* What are you doing?"

"Please, just hang on, sweetheart. I'll explain in a second." With that he threw the vehicle into reverse and jammed the accelerator to the floorboard.

The MRAP responded with a throaty roar as it lurched backwards, throwing Sheila up against the steering wheel.

Bubba kept his eyes on the thugs in the parking lot via the mirror. They'd released the aging cheerleader who made her way toward the armory. One of the two slipped behind the wheel as the other crammed the trophy in the backseat. Creep number two barely had time to climb in and shut the door before Bubba closed the distance between them.

The heavy, explosive-resistant, armored personnel carrier was still gathering speed when it slammed into the front end of the gunmen's Japanese import with a crunch and squeal that Bubba found profoundly satisfying.

"Dear God!" Sheila gasped after being tossed the short distance from the steering wheel back into his chest. "What have you done?"

"I stopped a robbery," he said. "Stopped that sucker cold."

She stared at him in utter shock. "What are you talking about? What's—"

"C'mon," he said, leveraging her up and out of his lap. "We've gotta get moving. They might get away."

"Who?" she asked, still befuddled. "I don't understand Will. *Will?*"

Busy getting untangled, he didn't want to take the time for explanations. "Just stay here for a bit. Don't come out unless I call for you."

"What? Why? Geez, Will—you're scaring me!"

"I know, and I'm sorry. I'll explain. Just— Just don't go anywhere."

He shoved the door open and rolled out of the truck. After pushing the door closed behind him, he raced toward the collision.

The sight which greeted him brought an instant smile. Neither thug had worn a seat belt, and when the impact triggered the airbags in their car, both got a hearty smack in the face--all compliments of the federal government's guidelines for automobile safety.

The man who'd gotten in last also got the worst of it. His nose had been smashed sideways by the impact, and his eyes had rolled up in his head. Blood seeped down his shirt front. The driver hadn't fared much better, but he remained conscious, and though groggy, appeared determined to get his door open.

Bubba figured that option was highly unlikely as the MRAP had not only given the front end of the car a distinct accordion look, it caused both front doors to buckle. Try as they might, neither man would be leaving the car soon. The doors would almost certainly have to be pried open. As a firefighter trainee, Bubba had a little experience with a tool the newspapers called the "Jaws of Life." It would almost certainly be needed, but not until someone with a badge and a gun made sure the bad guys wouldn't come out shooting.

He couldn't understand why no one had left the armory in pursuit of the gunmen. As he wandered toward the building, Sheila peeked out from the passenger side door and called to him. "Can I come out now? Is it safe?"

"Yeah," he said, "I— I'm still trying to wrap my head

around all this."

"All what?" she asked as he helped her out of the MRAP. She began to answer her own question when she saw the crushed car and the two men inside.

"Help!" yelled the wizened cheerleader from the double doors of the armory. "They chained it shut!"

As the wail of sirens grew, Bubba again climbed into the National Guard vehicle and worked his way to the back where he knew an assortment of tools had been stashed. He prayed for a bolt cutter.

He heard Sheila shout, "Oh my God, Will, a guy in the car has a gun!"

"Hide!" he yelled back. "You'll be okay. He can't get out." *At least, I hope like hell he can't get out.* Bubba focused on extracting the bolt cutters from the footlocker-sized toolbox.

Once he had the tool in hand, he made his way to the front and got out. Sheila crouched on the pavement near a rear tire, a worried look on her face. Bubba dropped down beside her to give her a hug. "You'll be fine, sweetheart. Just stay here. Or better yet, get back in the MRAP. I've gotta go cut the chain off the armory door."

As he jogged toward the older woman standing outside the building, two cars from the Charles County Sherriff's Department swooped into the lot and squealed to a stop beside the wreckage. Both officers emerged with their weapons drawn.

Bubba felt a huge swell of pride. He'd taken out two bad guys in one fell swoop, and no one had gotten hurt. The emotion gave him added strength as he bore down on the handles of the bolt cutter. He had to make two cuts to one of the links before the chain with its heavy padlock rattled onto the sidewalk.

When the door was pushed open from the inside, the first face he saw belonged to Colonel Lovejoy, commander of the 108th Forward Support Group.

He did not look happy.

~*~

Willa Mae sat on the concrete floor next to Ramona and tried to comfort her as the EMTs tended to Odell who had been knocked unconscious by one of the gunmen. "I'm sure he'll be all right. Didn't you tell me he was hardheaded?" She followed the question with a huge smile.

It seemed to work as Ramona responded with a brief chuckle. "He is, about some things. It's just—" She stopped talking when Odell's eyes fluttered open, and he responded to the smelling salts in the EMT's hand.

"Easy, pardner," said the emergency worker. "Just relax and let us check you out."

"What happened?" he asked, reaching toward the back of his head. He winced when he touched a lump that had formed there.

"We need to get you to the ER and have someone look at the back of your head. You probably have a concussion. Now, without moving your head, see if you can follow my hand."

Willa Mae watched as the lawman followed instructions.

He reached toward Ramona and patted her arm. "I'll be okay."

"He's probably right," said the EMT, "but even if he were a doctor himself, we wouldn't take his word for it. Do you want to ride along in the ambulance?"

"Absolutely," she said.

"So, who whacked me, and why?"

Ramona gave him a quick recap of what they knew. She complimented Bubba's quick thinking and the speedy arrival of Odell's deputies. "They have it all under control."

"What about the derby?" Odell asked. "Is it over?"

"Nope," said Willa Mae. "We've still got a little way to go to reach the halfway point and award the trophy." She turned toward Ramona. "I know that's your department, but if you need me to, I can stumble my way through the presentation."

"You'd better stick around," Odell said. "This is your show, Ramona. It wouldn't be right for you to run off in the middle of it."

Ramona looked anything but happy with the suggestion.

"C'mon, girl," said Willa Mae. "You've gotta give me a chance to catch up with you on the track. I haven't scored a single point all night." They helped each other stand, a process made trickier because of their roller skates and bruises.

Ramona frowned. "I'm worried. Odell is—"

"Gonna be fine," he said.

One of the EMTs interrupted them. "We need to get moving," he said. They helped Odell stand and escorted him to the ambulance. The two women trailed close behind.

"Go on now," Odell said as they loaded him into the vehicle. "You've got more important things to do than hold my hand."

Ramona clambered up beside him, gave him a kiss, and dropped back down to the driveway. "Okay," she said, "but only because you insist."

"I do. Now get back in there and take charge. You know you want to!"

"Oh, yeah," Ramona whispered as the ambulance pulled away. "I just love being the boss and watching someone I love taken to the hospital without me."

Willa Mae pulled her gently back into the armory. "He's tough. A little bump on the head won't slow him down much. And besides, the sooner we're done here, the sooner you can go be with him."

"I know, but it just doesn't seem fair."

"Fair?" Willa Mae shook her head. "I don't think fair has ever been part of the deal. Seems like someone always ends up doing more than everyone else. Leastwise, that's the way it's been in every organization I've been part of."

Ramona shrugged. "I know." She took a deep breath. "Okay, let's get this party started."

"Or restarted."

They high-fived each other and skated directly back to the track. Most of the crowd had reassembled since the deputies and the ambulance no longer provided a show. Ramona signaled to the announcer to get things cranked up again which he did with a flair.

"Due to the interruption in our match, we've reset the clock," he announced. His words got the crowd's attention. "Now we're ready to go. We're about to start our final jam of the first half. Ladies, take your positions!"

Willa Mae once again found herself on the track beside Ramona, mouth guard in place and limbs bent, ready for the start. Moments later, both women raced toward the first turn moving as quickly as they could to catch up with the blocker. and do their best to break through.

For once, Willa Mae got lucky. She found an opening between two of her teammates and raced through. Though roughly bumped by an all-business blocker from the Hip Hops, she stayed on her skates and charged ahead. A jam only lasted two minutes, but that one little taste of success gave her a jolt of renewed energy. She pressed even harder to try and break through again.

Ramona, it seemed, couldn't make any headway at all. Blocked at every attempt, she seemed disheartened. That quickly changed when Willa Mae caught up to her and gave her a solid shoulder bump.

It seemed to supercharge Ramona who responded with a hip thrust that almost sent Will Mae off the track. After that, they focused on the blockers and worked their way forward.

All too soon the jam ended, and they skated to their respective benches. Willa Mae turned around and worked her way back to Ramona's side of the track. "You really know how to throw your hips around, girl!"

"I try," Ramona said, still trying to catch her breath.

Willa Mae pointed to the area set aside for the trophy. "I think it's time we explained about that, don't you?"

"As soon as someone puts the trophy back."

~*~

Sheila's anger grew as she watched some jerk in an army uniform giving Will an earful for his "unauthorized use of a military vehicle." The officer kept repeating something about the Guard not being involved in local law enforcement.

After they examined the wrecked car still pinned beneath the MRAP, the officer ordered Will to move the army vehicle so he could inspect it for damage.

When she could stand watching it no longer, Sheila forced open a rear door of the crushed car and retrieved the outlandish trophy. Though ungainly, it wasn't too heavy for her to carry, so she hauled it back into the armory and set it back on its pedestal. Very few people seemed to notice, and she realized if someone wanted to steal the stupid thing, the perfect time to do it had arrived.

But, since it obviously meant a lot to Will, she wasn't about to let that happen. She took up a position halfway between the trophy and the exit where she could keep an eye on both. If there was any justice in the world, Will would come sauntering through those doors any minute.

In the meantime, she turned her attention toward the two women running the derby. She'd come to like Ramona; the woman seemed both honest and frank, and it didn't hurt that she never talked down to Will. She treated him like the decent guy Sheila knew him to be, even if the stiff-necked National Guard officer disagreed. She doubted he even knew how to crank up an MRAP much less back one up on an instant's notice in order to foil a robbery. She remained proud of her hero no matter what anyone else said.

Though some of the patrons remained focused on the skaters and clustered around them near the track, a fair number had wandered over to the trophy and listened while Ramona and her friend from the county garden club spoke. They explained a last-minute rule change for awarding the Hildegard Henderson Horticultural trophy.

Ramona went first. "Because there were some awful things done by a disgruntled individual, several of the gardeners involved in the contest were robbed of their ability to compete. In light of that we've decided to hold the trophy this year. It will remain on display in the Convention Center. We will post a framed certificate naming all of this year's competitors as First Place Winners of this year's event."

This engendered a good bit of chatter within the crowd, most especially among those who also belonged to the garden clubs.

Willa Mae then chimed in. "As many of you know, the award also includes a generous allowance for landscaping services." She pointed to Ramona's son who stood in her shadow smiling and trying not to appear overly nervous. "Donny Dorn here will oversee that work and the required scheduling. Those services will also be shared by everyone who entered the contest."

As the two women went on to congratulate the winners and thank all the many companies and individuals who helped stage the event, Sheila turned her attention back to the armory entrance. Will still hadn't shown up.

Someone else caught her eye instead. A tall figure wearing a hoodie emerged from the room where volunteers were counting the proceeds from the event. A hooded sweatshirt worn during a South Georgia summer made about as much sense as a snake wearing a tutu. Something was clearly off.

"Hey!" she yelled, moving cautiously in his direction.

He paused and looked up at her, then took off running.

In that one brief moment, Sheila realized two things. He had bundles of cash in each hand, and she knew who he was. She would recognize Monty's face anywhere. The brazen jackass was back!

The door to the room where the accounting had taken place was shut, so she couldn't tell if anyone inside had been hurt. She was torn between chasing Monty and checking on the volunteers in the closed room. She had to act fast and prayed Will might see the creep leave the building. Maybe he could run him over with the MRAP, too!

"Ramona, help," she screamed as she ran toward the counting room. "It's Monty! He's stealing the playground money!"

~*~

Ramona heard Sheila's yell and turned in time to see her dash toward the counting room. "Aw geez," she groaned.

Willa Mae was similarly alarmed. "Twice in one night? *Come on!*"

"Gangway," yelled Ramona as the two of them set off in pursuit of the thief. Fans separated quickly to let them through, and a number joined them in the chase.

"You *know* this Monty character?" Willa Mae asked as they charged through the armory's double doors and whizzed past Col. Lovejoy who looked as if he'd just been goosed.

"I only know him by his reputation," Ramona breathed, still intent on the man trying to run away from them. "But his grandma's a piece of work."

"Well, he's a piece of sumpthin," Willa Mae observed.

A getaway meant Monty had to run toward the opening in the gate which enclosed the National Guard property. A bench at the entrance was occupied by Annabelle Knox and her son, a heavy-set man in his 50s who was trying to comfort her.

"Stop that man!" Ramona yelled to him as she and Willa Mae redoubled their efforts. They were gaining on the thief, but it wouldn't be long before he reached the road. Ramona guessed he'd left his car running, assuming

Constance hadn't volunteered to be his driver.

Annabelle's son stood and moved toward the center of the drive. In response, Monty angled to one side, then shifted back the other way, like a football runner trying to dodge a defender. He didn't see Annabelle stand up, too.

Please, Annabelle, don't try anything stupid. Let him go. We'll get him.

The expression on the face of the seventy-something cheerleader said everything. Tired of being pushed around and used as a human shield, she set her sights on the man running toward her.

"Monty! Stop, now! Don't—"

Before she could finish, Annabelle slapped the middle of Monty's face. He staggered to a stop, pawing at his nose with a bundle of cash still clutched in his hand. Before he could retaliate or continue his escape, Annabelle's son grabbed him by the shoulder and jerked him around.

The delay provided just enough time for Ramona and Willa Mae to catch up. Ramona put on the brakes, but Willa Mae didn't. She slammed into Monty at top speed, took him down hard, and landed on top of him.

Ramona and Annabelle's son quickly recovered the stolen money which Monty released when he hit the pavement. He moved his arms and legs sluggishly and moaned.

Ramona approached Anabelle with concern. "Are you all right? Did you hurt your hand?"

"I'm fine," she said, revealing the heavy padlock she'd used on Monty's face. "I felt like I needed something to defend myself with." She looked down at the man she'd stopped. "Do you think he'll be all right?"

"Can't say I care," replied Ramona.

"Somebody needs to call the police," Willa Mae said as she shifted around and positioned herself on Monty's chest.

"I already did that," said a slender woman as she walked toward them from outside the gate.

Ramona thought she recognized her voice, but the speaker appeared only vaguely familiar. "Do I know—"

"I'm Alexis Rae," the woman said with a wink. "And his is the second time tonight I've called 911. I imagine that's some kind of record."

Chapter Fifteen

"I do not believe in using women in combat, because females are too fierce." – Margaret Mead

Odell savored the smell of bacon, eggs, and English toast emanating from the plate of goodies the waitress had just delivered. It seemed a fitting reward after having spent the night in the Charles County hospital. Ramona arrived a couple hours after he was admitted and didn't react well when told he wouldn't be released until morning. But then he hadn't reacted well, either.

She had insisted that they go out for breakfast as soon as he was discharged. He gave in not knowing she had invited his nephew and Sheila to join them. The younger couple sat across from them, admiring the food on their plates.

"Ram-moan-ah told me what you two did last night," Odell said. "I couldn't be more proud of you. I spoke to my contact in the GBI, and he feels certain the two guys you stopped were the ones who murdered Leonard Henderson and wrecked so many small businesses. Thank you for doing my job for me."

"It was all Will's doing," Sheila said, leaning even closer to him. "He's a hero."

"I agree, but from what I hear, Col. Killjoy wasn't too pleased," said Ramona.

Bubba nodded. "Not at first, anyway. He was pretty mad. Kept threatening to have me court-martialed."

"For saving the day?" Odell asked.

"For putting a dent in the MRAP—"

"*What?*"

"—among other things."

Sheila quickly chimed in. "He changed his tune though, when a bunch of folks came to shake Will's hand and thank him for taking out two armed men without putting anyone else in danger." She aimed a thousand-watt smile at him. "Like I said, he's a hero."

Bubba looked embarrassed and pointed at Ramona. "I heard *you* nabbed the guy who tried to rob the derby."

Ramona laughed. "I chased him, but my friend Willa Mae took him down. That might not have happened if Annabelle Knox hadn't softened him up first." She shook her head. "She's the sweetest old gal you'd ever hope to meet, but she packs a pretty mean punch."

Odell grinned. "You'll be happy to know ol' Monty gave up his grandmother, too."

Ramona gasped. "Connie was involved in the robbery?"

"No. But Monty said she paid him to spread the weed killer." He chuckled. "What a weasel. I suspect my staff has made sure everyone in the jailhouse knows he got stopped dead in his tracks by a seventy-eight-year-old cheerleader. Can we give her a medal?"

"That would be really cute," Ramona said, "but wouldn't want to embarrass her."

"She might think of it as a reward," suggested Sheila.

"Oh!" Ramona put her hand to her forehead. "Speaking of rewards... I almost forgot." She dug into her purse and extracted a small envelope which she handed to Bubba. "You have a secret admirer. After all the fuss last night, she told me how pleased she was by what you did and asked me to give you that as a thank you."

Bubba opened the envelope and let the contents roll out onto the table: two, shiny gold coins, just like the ones he and Sheila had brought to Ramona. He looked up at her in surprise. "These aren't part of the donation to the playground fund, are they? I couldn't—"

"Nope. I promise. Those are for you. The lady who gave them to me said it was 'a token of her esteem.'"

"Who was it?" Odell asked.

"She prefers to remain anonymous."

"I know just what I'll do with these," Bubba said brightly, turning toward Sheila. "We ought to be able to swap 'em for a really nice wedding ring."

"I don't need anything fancy," she said. "Keep it simple. We'll save the money for the nursery."

Odell sat back in surprise. "You two are—"

"Gonna get married," Bubba said. "And we're going to have a family, too."

"That— That's great! A wedding."

Ramona and Odell exchanged looks. "I love the idea," she said.

"I do, too." Odell gave her a squeeze. "And I'm not just talking about a wedding for them."

Alexis Rae turned off the television set in her stateroom aboard the *SS Mystic*, a small but elegant cruise ship on the first leg of a multi-country voyage. She was immensely pleased by the news that a joint effort of local and federal law enforcement agencies had resulted in several dozen arrests and the elimination of a notorious drug cartel. No mention was made of St. Charlotte, but she knew who was involved.

Finally able to relax, she looked forward to dinner that evening. As the sole occupant of the ship's most luxurious suite, she had automatically been invited to dine with Karl Hasdahl, the ship's Captain. By all accounts, he was a handsome and well-respected bachelor just about her own age.

Alexis adjusted her hair in the mirror, pleased with the result. It was time to begin the first phase of her new life.

~End~

About the Author

Josh Langston's fiction has been published in a variety of magazines and anthologies, and both his Christmas and Western short story collections have reached the Amazon top 20 for genre fiction. His many novels are split between historical fiction and, with the exception of this title and one other, contemporary fantasy.

Josh also loves to teach. His classes on novel writing, memoir, and independent publishing are filled with students eager to learn and have their work perused by a pro. His textbooks on the craft of fiction, memoir, and novel writing provide a humorous and easy-to-understand approach to the subjects while imparting valuable tips and techniques. **Naked Notes!** is the fourth title in his textbook series and was released in 2018.

Josh loves to chat with book clubs and can be reached via email at: **DruidJosh@gmail.com**. Be sure to visit his website, too: **www.JoshLangston.com**

~*~

Now, turn the page for an added bonus: Chapter One of **Resurrection Blues**, a story about a little Alabama town which, as far as the county, state, and federal government are concerned, doesn't exist....

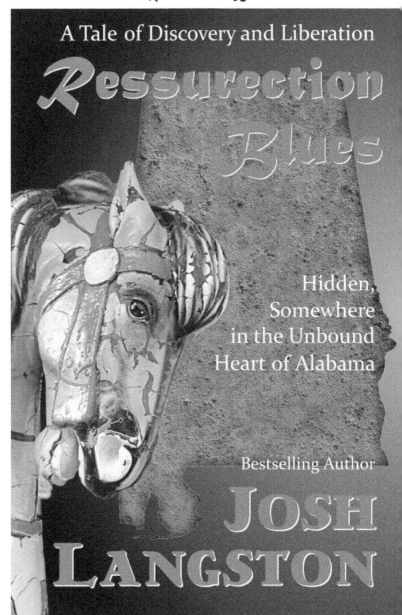

A Tale of Discovery and Liberation

Ressurrection

Blues

Hidden,
Somewhere
in the Unbound
Heart of Alabama

Bestselling Author

JOSH
LANGSTON

Resurrection Blues

Chapter One

"One good fire is the equivalent of three good moves."
–Wayne A. Langston

Trey opened his door to the first line of a joke: *An Indian, a dwarf, and a biker walk into a bar...* Except he didn't own a bar, and this clearly wasn't a joke.

"We're lookin' for Trey Bowman," the Indian said.

"As in A. A. Bowman, the third," added the biker.

Trey looked down at the dwarf, expecting her to add something. She didn't. Instead, she stunned him with the sexiest smile he'd ever seen. He dragged his gaze from her face and quickly inspected the other two visitors. They appeared calm, and unarmed. *Always a good sign.* Still....

"He's dead," Trey said.

"Then, who the hell're you?" asked the Indian, "And why are you in his house?"

"Who the hell are *you*, and why do you want to know?"

The biker looked less likeable than he had before, the morphing process moving him from possible miscreant to probable felon. "It's important we find Trey Bowman. He's not in any trouble. Leastwise, not with us, but if he's dead we'll need to see proof."

"Like a grave?" Trey asked.

"More like a body," said the Indian. "But a death certificate would probably do."

The dwarf continued to smile, but the effect ceased to be sexy. It now seemed morbidly curious--the sort of smile reserved for really bad traffic accidents, or public executions.

"You didn't answer my questions," Trey said, shifting his foot slightly in order to get more of it wedged at the bottom of the door. "So, again: who are you, and why are you looking for Trey Bowman?"

"Augie sent us," the tiny female said, her voice a delicious tinkling of fine crystal.

"Augie who?"

"Augie Bowman."

"*He's still alive?*"

"Yeah, but not for long. Doc says he's only got a few days left." The Indian looked down at a photo in his hand, then held it up to eye level and glanced back and forth between Trey's face and the picture. "He sent us to find you."

Trey squinted at him. "Okay, *I'm* Augustus Bowman."

"The third," said the biker by way of confirmation. 'Your grampaw said you go by 'Trey.'"

"I do, but he barely even knows me," Trey said, twisting to see if he recognized himself in the photo. He hadn't seen his grandfather in at least twenty years.

"Why don't you call yourself 'Augustus' or 'Augie'?" the biker asked. "Don't you like your name?"

"I like Trey."

"I expected someone more... I dunno, interesting," said the Indian to the biker. "This guy's a geek."

"I am not a geek! I-- I hate computers."

"Relax, sweetie," said the diminutive femme. "He's not talkin' about the kinda geek you're thinkin' of." She looked up at her companions. "I think it's him, but we'd better check his ID just to be sure."

"*My ID?* This is my *house*, for cryin' out loud. I don't have to produce an ID. You should be showing me yours."

"I'm Warren Lightfoot," said the Indian, pushing his arm between the door and the jamb. "You can call me Bud." He gripped Trey's hand firmly, shook it once, then let go.

"Bud. Right." Trey looked at the biker.

"I'm Dago," he said, keeping his hands in the pockets of his jeans.

"Of course you are," Trey said, utterly clueless. He looked down. "And you must be...."

"The Virgin Mary," she said with an absolutely straight face.

He tried to roll with it. "Would it be okay if I just called you 'Mary'?"

"Sure," she said, relighting her ten-thousand-watt smile. "I'm not really a virgin."

"Good," he said. "I mean, about your name. Not the, you know--"

"Time to go," said Dago.

Oddly, Trey felt no threat from the bizarre trio. Something about them had the ring of truth, and he felt compelled to go with them. Besides, he'd already made a complete mess of his life, and he clearly had nothing better to do.

"You got a car?" Bud asked. "We've got a truck, but somebody'd have to ride in the back."

"Not me!" Mary said. She pushed through the door and grabbed Trey's hand. "You wouldn't make a lady sit in the back of a truck, would ya?" She snuggled up to his thigh, and batted what he suddenly realized were absurdly long eyelashes.

"I've got a car," he said. "I can follow you."

Bud smiled for the first time. "Good, then let's get movin.'"

"Waitaminute!" Trey said. "First things first. How long am I gonna be gone? Do I need to pack some clothes? Leave a forwarding address? Who's gonna feed my parakeet?"

"Good Lord, he's got a tweety," said the Indian. "I told you he was a geek."

"Bring the bird," Mary said. "And throw some clothes in a bag. If you need more later, I'm sure we can find the hole and come back."

"*'Find the hole?'* What the hell are you talkin' about?"

The biker stared at Mary as if he was contemplating dwarficide.

"It's just an expression," Bud said. "We'll explain later."

Trey looked down at Mary. "I don't really have a parakeet."

"I can get you one."

"No. That's cool. I don't--"

"You like blue or yellow? Green, maybe? I think that's all the colors they come in. But I can check it out." She pulled him after her. "Where's your bedroom?"

Trey hit the brakes. Mary may have been short, but she had full grown curves. "My bedroom?"

"Yeah. Unless you keep your clothes somewhere else."

"Oh. Right. I thought--"

"You have a dirty mind, Trey." She laughed, and somewhere a shelf full of exquisitely fragile glass toppled onto the floor. "Where's your suitcase?"

He retrieved it from his closet, then paused long enough to look for Mary's companions. "Where are--"

"Outside."

"While we're--"

"In here. Packing." On her tiptoes, she groped blindly in the top drawer of his dresser and withdrew a handful of briefs. "I figured you for boxers." She threw them on the unmade bed, then continued foraging in his other drawers. T-shirts and socks followed the underwear and landed in a pile.

Trey stuffed his clothes into the travel bag as quickly as Mary launched them in his direction. "Jeans and sweatshirts are in the closet," he said, but she had already discovered them. "Will I need a jacket?"

She paused to look at him, curiosity coloring her classic features. "I doubt it. Unless we've slipped into another dimension, this is still summer in Atlanta, isn't it?"

"But I don't know where we're going!"

"West and north, but not far either way."

"That's comforting."

"These are nice," she said, throwing a pair of loafers at him. "Bring 'em."

"Those are my formal sorta shoes. They're a little tight."

"Wear 'em for me, then."

"Okay," he said. "Listen, I'll get the rest of that."

"No, you won't. We're done. You got that stuff packed yet?"

Very little space remained in the valise. "Uh--"

"Don't forget your hairdryer, razor, and toothbrush."

"Why do I get the feeling you've done this before?"

"I've got six brothers," she said. "Most of 'em are younger than me, but none of 'em know how to pack. It's just not a guy-thing, y'know?"

He nodded. She was right. She was also leaving.

He zippered the case and hauled it out of the room as Mary walked out the front door. With none of his visitors in sight, Trey slipped into the little pantry in his kitchen and reached into the flour container where he kept his emergency fund--a roll of twenties he'd received in exchange for a motorcycle he couldn't afford to keep running. The money was gone.

Trey looked up at a chuckle from just outside the pantry.

Bud held up his cash, still wrapped in a plastic bag. "Lookin' for this?"

"How'd--"

"You'd be surprised how many people hide their money like that," he said, tossing it to him. "You oughta find a safer spot."

"Like the freezer?"

"Nah. I'd have found it there, too."

Trey felt violated. "Where, then?"

"I like banks," he said. "You ready to go?"

"Do I have a choice?"

"Not really."

They left.

~*~

Willard Calcraft had more attaboys and fewer friends than anyone else in the Internal Revenue's regional office in Atlanta. Nicknamed "The Executioner" by some wag who discovered a similarly named 19th century English hangman, Will hadn't actually killed anyone, though it was generally believed his unrelenting zeal for collecting back taxes had caused several clients to come after *him*.

His wife, Marjorie, had other reasons for wanting him dead. Foremost among them was a tax evader named

Anastasia Jones whose profession required the strategic removal of her costume while dancing. Will had racked up some serious overtime on that case.

He had no idea Marjorie was contemplating his demise, but then few of her ideas had ever successfully garnered his attention. His inability to recognize problems of the domestic variety left him free to concentrate on his professional duties, such as the file in his hand.

A single sheet of paper occupied the folder. The name on the neatly typed file tab read: *Bowman, Augustus A*. The document contained the first clues in the kind of trail Willard Calcraft had followed often. He smiled in anticipation.

There was a "Bowman, Augustus A." listed as the President of the Resurrection Holding Company, the address a rural route somewhere in Alabama. There was also a "Bowman, Augustus A." listed as the pastor of the Resurrection Free Will Unitarian Universalist Mission. It bore the exact same rural route address as the Resurrection Holding Company. He loved it when tax cheats tried to hide behind religion and considered himself duly constituted to collect that which was due unto Caesar, but not necessarily because he had a thing for Caesar. A final entry showed the results of a search for a personal income tax return for the head of the two organizations: all blanks.

Will swiveled his chair around to face a wall map of his region, Alabama, and quickly browsed through a listing of all the municipalities therein. A couple of town names came close, but Resurrection was not to be found. He obtained the zip code for the rural route, located the area in the hilly terrain of the state's rugged northern reaches and hunted for something that may have lent its name to both a trading company and a church. After twenty minutes of close scrutiny, he abandoned the map search without learning anything new. His curiosity growing, Will typed the vaguely Indian-sounding word "Resurrection" into his favorite Internet search engine and aside from religious entries, came up empty once again.

Rather than antagonize his contacts so late in the day, Will decided to leave the mystery of Resurrection until the next morning. That would give him plenty of time to pay Anastasia a visit before he drove home. He cleared off his desk, made sure he had an ample supply of dollar bills in his pocket, and left.

~*~

Mary rode with Trey as they angled northwest away from Atlanta. She made herself comfortable on top of his travel bag. Trey tried not to stare at the harness strap of her seat belt which neatly bisected her breasts.

"They don't make these damn things for little people," she said. "Driving anything bigger than a bumper car is a real pain in the ass."

"I'd be more sympathetic if I knew where we were going."

"Resurrection, of course."

"Of course," he echoed. He remembered the name, usually spoken under his mother's breath and always referenced in the negative. According to her, Hell was a kinder, gentler alternative. "My mother told me some interesting stories about Resurrection. She wasn't a big fan."

"It's not a place for everyone," Mary said, "but I wouldn't live anywhere else."

"*Have* you lived anyplace else?"

She glanced at him with a slightly pained expression. "I've vacationed elsewhere. Or tried to. Vacation is over-rated. Frankly, I prefer stayin' at home." She pointed at Bud's truck some distance ahead. "Don't lose sight of them."

He increased his speed. "What's so special about Resurrection?"

"It's hard to explain."

"I've got nothin' but time."

"It's something you have to experience. The town isn't much to look at. It's more like your favorite jeans rather than your church clothes."

"I'm not much of a church-goer," Trey said. "None of my family was."

"That's not true. Augie lives next to the church. He's a minister."

Trey felt his eyebrows scrunch together. "Augie Bowman, *a preacher?* Maybe I'm not your guy after all. My grandfather was--"

"*Is.* He's not dead, yet."

"--is a con artist. According to my mother. As I recall she also called him a snake oil salesman and a carnival barker. There were some others, too, but those are the ones that stand out."

Mary squinted at him. "Your Mom told you that?"

"Yeah."

"Sure doesn't sound like Augie. She must not have known him very well. Either that, or he's changed. Drastically. The Boss is... The Boss! He's probably one of the smartest men in the world." Mary tried to cross her arms, but the combination of breasts and harness made it tricky. "I don't mean 'smart' like brain surgeon smart. He's smart in practical ways. He makes things work. He's not only a minister--"

"What church would have him?"

"Unitarian."

"Figures."

"He's also the banker."

"*The* banker?" Trey asked. "You make it sound like there's only one."

"That's all we need."

"A con artist owns the town's only bank?" He chuckled. These people were deranged. His mother couldn't have been that wrong about his grandfather, even if she did tend to be a tad over-reactive. "What a set up. He doesn't even have to drive his little lambs to the shed. They line up to be fleeced all by themselves."

"Are you this cynical about everything?"

He shook his head. "Only about cons, and I've gotta tell ya, that's exactly what this feels like."

She looked puzzled. "We're not tryin' to trick you."

"Right," he said, reaching into the glove box to extract a map. He tossed it in her lap. "Why don't you show me where Resurrection is on that?"

She leaned forward and put the map back. "'Cause I can't."

"You can't read a map?"

"I can't show you where Resurrection is, 'cause it's not on that map. It's not on *any* map."

"Because it doesn't exist. It's a scam." He slowed the car and looked for a place to turn around.

"What are you doing?"

"Goin' back," he said. "I've got more important things to do than waste my time with lunatics."

"Okay. But what about me? I don't want to go to Atlanta. I wanna go home."

"Fine," he said, flashing his lights as he pulled off the road. The tires crunched in the red clay and gravel of the narrow shoulder. Well ahead of him, the pickup truck slowed then did a U-turn and sped back toward them. "You can ride back with Dago and Crazy Horse," he said.

"Warren Lightfoot. Bud."

"Whatever."

She frowned at him. "You're a real asshole, you know that? I thought you might be a decent guy, like your grandfather, but I was wrong."

"I *am* a decent guy," he said. "I just don't like being jerked around, and that's all you've been doing."

The pickup pulled off the road opposite Trey's car. Bud rolled the window down. "What's the problem?"

Mary leaned across Trey and called back, "He wants to go home. He thinks we're tryin' to pull something over on him."

Bud jammed the shift lever into park and killed his engine. His door squealed as he opened it and again when he pushed it shut. He jogged across the road and leaned down to look through Trey's window. "So, you don't want to see your grandfather. He's on his deathbed. It's his last wish, on Earth. But you're too busy to see the old guy off?"

"I think you're trying to pull some kind of scam."

"Like what?"

"I dunno. I'm not the con artist; my grandfather is. And, I suspect, y'all are, too."

Bud pursed his lips and went silent for a long moment. "Why would we bother to scam someone who's broke?"

"Who said I was broke?"

"The Boss."

"I'm not broke!"

"Really? That's odd, 'cause according to Augie, you've been unemployed for almost a year. Your last three checks bounced like Texas Leaguers, and your credit report shows more red ink than black. A lot more. Your bank's going to take your house at the end of the month."

Trey squeaked, "You ran a credit check on me?"

"I didn't. The Boss did. He said he had to wait until you were ready."

"Ready for what?"

"A change," said Mary. "Or would you rather go back to the same old, same old? At least until someone comes along to take it away."

"Now wait just a damn minute--"

"Not us," Mary said, "the bank."

"But--"

"Don't get us wrong," Bud said. "We aren't above trying to pull a fast one on some fat-cat outsider. You're more like family."

"How comforting."

"Don't get drippy on us," Bud said. "Can we go now? I wanna get home before dark."

"Yeah, sure, but I'm not promising I'll stay."

Bud didn't respond. He walked back to his truck, fired it up and gunned the engine through the turn which took him back the way he'd come. Trey pulled out after him.

"No one has to stay in Resurrection," Mary said. "It's not a prison. The people who live there like it there. Give it a chance; you might like it, too. If not, we'll show you the way out."

"I doubt you'll have to show me," he said.

Mary only smiled.

~*~

Marjorie Calcraft propped her chin on her knuckles and blew a strand of limp, blonde hair straight up off her forehead. Her closest friend, Alyson Spencer, topped off her cosmo, then carefully emptied the shaker into her own glass. "Drink up. The kids'll be home from practice soon."

Marjorie nodded despondently. "It's Tuesday, right? Excitement night."

"You goin' out for dinner?"

"We never go out anymore. Will says it's not cost effective."

"He actually says that?"

Marjorie shrugged. "No, but that's the way he acts. I'm tellin' ya, Aly, I can't take much more."

"Then divorce him. You're still a good-looking woman. You could find someone else, someone who'd appreciate you for who you are."

"Oh, right. I'm sure there are loads of handsome, single, well-to-do guys looking for fortyish blondes in size 12 slacks."

"You're a *12?*" Alyson asked, the skepticism in her voice barely contained.

Marjorie's lips twisted to the side. "Sometimes. Depends on the label."

"You could settle for less than perfect. Single and well-to-do sounds pretty good. It'd help if they like kids."

"You're the one with kids, not me," Marjorie said. "You make it sound so... *mercenary.*" She swirled the pink beverage in her glass and just barely managed to keep it from sloshing over the edge. She preferred wine glasses, the big, trendy bubble style. The way Alyson made cosmos--half vodka, half cranberry juice, a splash of Cointreau--it only took one to relax her. Two usually put her in a mild state of euphoria. Two, in the bubble glasses, would put her in a coma. That evening, however, she felt nothing but depression. "I think maybe I'll just shoot him."

Alyson grinned. Marjorie knew she liked nothing better than a good conspiracy, especially if nothing ever came of it.

"Could be messy," Alyson said. "Noisy, too. You got a gun?"

"Will does. Somewhere."

"Know how to use it?"

"What's to know? They do it all the time on TV." Marjorie took another sip of her drink. "I could do it. I could lock him outta the house, and when he tried to break in, could blow his cheatin' little weenie off."

Alyson took a sharp breath. "You think he's cheating? Really? With who? Anyone I know? Wait! I'll bet I know." She gave her head a sympathetic shake. "It's that busty brunette in the house with the pool. What's her name? Sheila something. I've heard she sunbathes in the nude. Can you believe it?"

"It's not Sheila Sonderberg," Marjorie said. "She's at least ten years older than I am. She gives kids piano lessons fergodsake."

"Well, then, who is it? Anyone I know?"

"Not unless you frequent strip clubs."

Alyson's previous sharp intake of breath failed to compete with her latest. "Are you sure? How do you know?"

"I followed him one night. He's been acting strange lately. Even more than usual, if you can believe it. He gave me some ridiculous story about having to go to the office, but knew better."

"And he went to a *strip club?*"

Marjorie nodded, tears welling in both eyes. "It took me fifteen minutes to get there, and I waited for almost an hour. He walked right past me when he came out. Didn't even recognize my car! Never looked in my direction."

"Maybe it was work-related."

Marjorie gave her a look she usually reserved for only the most deserving dumb asses.

~*~

Trey and Mary had driven for about two hours when the pickup in front of them slowed to a stop on the side of the road. Dago hopped out and walked back to Trey's car with the setting sun at his back, framed by a pair of non-descript Appalachian foothills.

"I'll drive from here," he said.

"No thanks," said Trey. "I'm not tired."

"He's not worried about your safety," Mary said. "It's a security thing." She looked into the back seat. "You can stretch out back there."

Trey shook his head. "I'm not stretching out anywhere but right here, behind the wheel. Listen, I promise not to tell anyone where your goofy little town is, if that's what you're worried about."

"We're not worried," Dago said, pressing something cold and hard against Trey's neck.

When he woke, he found himself curled up on the back seat, the sole occupant of the vehicle. He sat up and looked around, expecting some sort of unpleasant side effect from the tranquilizer Dago must have used on him. Instead, he felt surprisingly clear-headed, as if he'd had a good night's sleep.

He felt as though he owed it to himself to be angry at his captors, but he wasn't. Whatever had knocked him out left him feeling awfully good, though he doubted he'd been asleep very long. The sun sat low in the sky, but it was far from dusk. He vowed to settle things with Dago the next time he saw him. And Mary, too. She could have warned him he was about to take a nap.

He exited the car which was parked behind a single large house, and stretched. The dwelling was no different than a thousand others he'd seen in small towns throughout the South. Someone was in the process of painting the place but it wasn't a rehabilitation effort. The house had obviously been well kept. A huge dog of indeterminate breed filled the top of the stairs leading to the back door. Trey hoped it was on a chain, though it didn't appear interested in him. It yawned, exposing saurian teeth and a long pink tongue. Trey decided not to venture too far from his car. The thought made him spin around and look at the ignition for his keys. They weren't in sight.

"Trey!" said a gravelly voice from the porch. "How in the hell are you, boy?"

An old man leaned against the porch rail, a smile on his pale face. A great mane of white hair and a full, matching beard gave the man a distinctly Clausian look, although his body would never pass for a jolly old elf.

"*Gramp?*"

"C'mon up here, boy," said the old man. "Lemme get a look at you."

Trey ambled to the bottom of the stairs but stopped when the gigantic canine lifted its head and stared at him.

The old man waved his arm impatiently. "C'mon up. Tiny won't hurt ya. He's got about as much energy as me, and that ain't sayin' much."

Tiny lowered his great head as Trey climbed the stairs and stepped over him. The dog never even blinked.

The old man grabbed Trey's proffered hand and pulled him into a hug. "God, how I've missed you! I was sorry to hear about your Mom. I wanted to attend the funeral, but the doctor wouldn't let me out of bed."

Pressed to arm's length, Trey examined his grandfather. Though thin and pale, he certainly didn't look as though he'd just crawled from his death bed. "They told me you were, uhm, pretty sick."

"I am. Gonna die soon, they say." He gave Trey a toothy smile.

"You don't sound very upset about it."

He shrugged. "We all have to go sooner or later. No sense worryin' about it." He clapped Trey on the shoulder. "Don't misunderstand. I'm not eager to leave the midway. I'll ride this carousel for a few more turns, but when it's time to climb on the next ride, I'll be ready."

"You think death is just another carnival ride?"

"Isn't it?"

"No! Death is... death. It means everything's over. Done. Endless nothing."

"I like the carnival ride theory better. It's hard to get excited about 'endless nothing.'"

Trey felt suddenly foolish. He slapped his forehead. "I-- I get carried away sometimes and forget when to keep my big mouth shut. I'm sorry."

The old man smiled. "Don't be. You're entitled to your opinion." He motioned toward an open door. "It's cooler inside. You hungry?"

"Actually, I was thinking of maybe drivin' back tonight."

"Then you'll need these," the elder Bowman said handing him his car keys. "But surely you can stay for dinner."

"You're not going to drug me again, are you?" He still wanted to give Dago a piece of his mind, but the aroma of fried chicken and fresh bread all but overpowered him.

The old man laughed. "I can't promise you won't get sleepy after you eat a big meal, but if you're determined to leave, no one's going to stop you. I'll see to it someone helps you get to the main road."

Trey followed his grandfather through the house toward the kitchen. All along the way the smells of cooking food grew stronger, and Trey's appetite grew as well. A young woman met them at the kitchen door, then led the old man to a chair at a built-in table. "Have a seat, Boss. Everything's ready."

"Kate, this is my grandson, Trey. The one I've been telling you about."

She smiled and extended a hand. Trey accepted it while examining her face. "You look so familiar."

Kate chuckled. "I understand you spent the afternoon with my big sister. Folks say we look alike."

"*Mary's* your 'big' sister?"

"Yeah. 'Cept her name's not Mary."

A wave of confusion crested over Trey. It must've shown on his face.

"Her real name's Ethyl. She likes to use a variety of names. Can't say I blame her."

"Ethyl?"

"Yeah, like at the gas station, ethyl or regular."

Trey still didn't understand. He looked to his grandfather for help. He responded while piling chicken on a plate and passing it to Trey by way of Kate. "Ethyl teaches history," he explained. "She was having trouble getting through to some of her students and decided to try something a little unconventional to get their attention."

"This was a couple years ago, and she was getting desperate," Kate said. "There aren't that many folks willing to pay for history lessons to begin with. She couldn't afford to lose any students."

Trey tried to concentrate on what they were saying, but the smell of fried chicken made it difficult. Kate put a fist-sized helping of mashed potatoes on his plate and puddled gravy in the middle. A trickle of the thick, fragrant liquid dripped down one crisp edge of the chicken.

"What'd she do that was so different?" Trey asked.

"They were studying ancient Egypt at the time," Trey's grandfather said. "She came to school dressed like Cleopatra."

"What a shock that must've been," Kate said. "She found a costume from the old show days--harem pants, a skimpy top, lots of jewelry and make-up--then she waltzed into class and introduced herself as the Queen of the Nile. Wouldn't say anything more until the students addressed her properly. Pretty soon they were asking questions and she was giving answers. I daresay those kids learned a lot. Then, when word got out about her skimpy costume--"

"Which took about ten minutes," the old man interjected.

"--a whole bunch of boys signed up for her class. She wouldn't let 'em in unless they agreed to stay the whole year, and paid in advance. She chose one new character a week after that, and just played the roles. I know--I helped her with a lot of the costumes. She got so good at it, and had so much fun doing it, that she let it slide over into her non-school life. She even wears the costumes when she's working at the café. Customers love it."

"I thought you said she was a teacher."

"She is. She's also a business owner. Co-owner actually. She and a friend run a pastry shop in town."

Trey nodded. "Do you know who she is this week?"

"Wait, don't tell me," said the old man, his food untouched. He clenched his eyes shut in concentration. They all sat in silence until he shook his head in defeat.

"Think Christmas," Trey said.

"*Mary!* Of course," Kate giggled. "Bet that took you by surprise. 'Course, she's hardly a virgin."

Feeling his role as a southern gentleman had been compromised somehow, Trey said, "I wish y'all wouldn't do that."

"Do what?"

"Tell me you're not virgins."

"Who said anything about me?" Kate asked, as she coolly met his gaze.

Trey chomped down on a fleshy drumstick and chewed to cover his discomfort. He couldn't remember the last time he'd tasted anything so flavorful.

~End of Excerpt~

Made in the USA
Coppell, TX
24 May 2022

78127535R00155